Catherine Spencer

THE MORETTI MARRIAGE

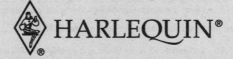

D0036142

HARLEQUIN®

TORONTO • NEW YORK • LONDON
AMSTERDAM • PARIS • SYDNEY • HAMBURG
STOCKHOLM • ATHENS • TOKYO • MILAN • MADRID
PRAGUE • WARSAW • BUDAPEST • AUCKLAND

ISBN 0-373-12474-0

THE MORETTI MARRIAGE

First North American Publication 2005.

Copyright © 2004 by Spencer Books Limited.

All rights reserved. Except for use in any review, the reproduction or utilization of this work in whole or in part in any form by any electronic, mechanical or other means, now known or hereafter invented, including xerography, photocopying and recording, or in any information storage or retrieval system, is forbidden without the written permission of the publisher, Harlequin Enterprises Limited, 225 Duncan Mill Road, Don Mills, Ontario, Canada M3B 3K9.

All characters in this book have no existence outside the imagination of the author and have no relation whatsoever to anyone bearing the same name or names. They are not even distantly inspired by any individual known or unknown to the author, and all incidents are pure invention.

This edition published by arrangement with Harlequin Books S.A.

® and TM are trademarks of the publisher. Trademarks indicated with ® are registered in the United States Patent and Trademark Office, the Canadian Trade Marks Office and in other countries.

www.eHarlequin.com

Printed in U.S.A.

"What are you really doing here, Nico?"

"Your mother invited me to attend your wedding."

"I don't believe you!" Chloe said. "Why would she do such a thing?"

"Because ours was the most civilized divorce in the world, so where is the harm in wishing you and this new man well and showing him he has nothing to fear from me?" Nico replied.

"He already knows that."

"Then my being here won't disturb him, will it?"

"Not a bit!"

"And what about you, Chloe? Will knowing I'm close by make you less sure of yourself and the plans you've made?"

"Absolutely not!"

"Then there's no problem."

"You are not coming to my wedding, and that's final! I'll see you in hell first!"

"Darling," he said lazily, "I've already spent enough time there."

Legally wed,
But he's never said
"I love you."

They're

The series where marriages are
made in haste…and love comes later….

Look out for more WEDLOCKED! wedding
stories available only from Harlequin Presents®

Coming in August 2005:
Blackmailed into Marriage
by Lucy Monroe
#2484

CHAPTER ONE

Friday, August 21

SUNLIGHT bounced off the swimming pool and patterned the bedroom ceiling with shifting reflections of the water. Another brilliant day in an endless summer that had left the grass scorched yellow except here, in her mother's garden, where in-ground sprinklers worked under cover of night to preserve the velvet-smooth emerald lawns.

It was after nine o'clock, a good two hours later than she usually awoke. But that tended to happen when a person had tossed restlessly throughout most of the night, unable to sleep. Now, lying flat on her back, with only a sheet to cover her, Chloe Matheson mentally reviewed the day ahead. The morning spent at the office, taking care of business, and a quick visit with Baron. Lunch with Monica, her best friend and matron of honor, followed by final dress fittings for both of them. One last meeting with the caterer, and a late afternoon consultation with her hair stylist. Then, as a grand finale, the cocktail party here at the house, to meet the groom's parents, newly arrived from Ottawa.

How had it happened that the small, intimate ceremony she and Baron had envisaged had turned into the social event of the season? How had a select guest list of twenty blossomed into something closer to a hundred and twenty?

They should have eloped, except that was something only the very young and impetuous did. She and Baron were too sensible, too mature, to act like Romeo and Juliet....

No! A door in her mind clanged firmly shut. *Not like Romeo and Juliet.* Chloe wanted no part of *anything* to do with them.

On the terrace below, her mother, Jacqueline, and grandmother, Charlotte, were taking breakfast. The low buzz of their conversation and the faint chink of china drifted through the open window, mingled with the aroma of coffee. Although she couldn't discern their actual words, Chloe knew they'd be discussing the wedding. It was all anyone talked about these days.

"You're making too much fuss about this," she'd objected, when the event had started to gather the speed of a runaway train. "It's not as if it's a first marriage for either Baron or me."

"If you care enough for one another to want to make it legal, then it's worth getting excited about," her mother had overruled. "And no daughter of mine is going to settle for some tacky little hole-and-corner wedding when I can afford to give her the best."

It hadn't seemed worth fighting about, back in April when Baron had proposed. Now though, Chloe wished she'd stood firm. But with the invitations sent out six weeks ago, all spare bedrooms in the house prepared for out-of-town guests, and every room at the nearby Trillium Inn reserved for the overflow, it was too late to apply the brakes.

Tucking a pillow behind her head, she glanced down at the silhouette of her body under the sheet. Her hip bones projected like clothespins anchored to her body by the concave dip of her abdomen. Her breasts lay so flat, they were barely discernible.

"Poached egg boobs are what we've got—the legacy of having nursed our babies," Monica had laughed, the day they'd gone shopping for wedding outfits. Then, realizing she'd stepped on tender ground, she'd sobered and said, "Sorry, Chloe, I forgot. I didn't mean to be insensitive."

Chloe, though, never forgot, and turning now to look at the silver-framed photograph on the nightstand, she met the solemn, dark-eyed gaze of her son, captured forever on film at two months. "Hey, angel," she whispered, her throat thick and aching.

Downstairs, the phone rang. With a tremendous effort, Chloe pulled herself back from the abyss of grief and regret forever waiting to swallow her up. Kissing her fingertip, she pressed it to her son's tiny mouth, curved in the beginnings of a gummy smile, then flung aside the sheet and headed for the shower.

Neither Jacqueline nor Charlotte heard her step out to the terrace, some twenty minutes later. They were too busy with their heads together, cooking up something so furtive that when Chloe said, calmly enough, "Good morning!" they sprang apart as if they'd been caught shoplifting.

"Darling!" her mother exclaimed, almost knocking over her coffee cup. "You're up! How…lovely!"

"I don't know what's so lovely about it, Mother," she replied, observing both women mistrustfully. "It's something we all do, every morning."

"But you look so *rested*," her grandmother chirped, which was an outright lie because Chloe knew very well that no amount of concealer had been able to disguise the smudged shadows under her eyes.

They were doing their very best to appear guileless, but something about their expressions—''smug'' was the word that sprang to Chloe's mind—made a mockery of their pathetic attempts to behave as if this were just another morning in the long week leading up to the wedding.

''All right,'' she said, plunking herself down at the breakfast table. ''Out with it. What's going on?''

They exchanged a shifty glance, then hurriedly broke eye contact. ''Well,'' her mother practically twittered, ''you have a dress fitting this afternoon, a meeting with the caterer—''

''I'm perfectly well aware of what's on *my* calendar,'' Chloe informed her testily. ''It's your agenda that worries me.''

Her grandmother bathed her in a sunny smile. ''Have you forgotten? We're entertaining Baron's parents tonight, and we want everything to be quite…perfect.'' She spooned fresh blueberries into a small crystal bowl and passed it to Chloe. ''After all, you never get a second chance to make a good first impression.''

''Exactly.'' Her mother poured her a cup of coffee. ''Don't look so suspicious, darling. What do you think is going on?''

''That you're both stonewalling me.'' Ignoring the blueberries, Chloe added a little cream to her coffee and stirred. ''Who was that on the phone earlier?''

''Nobody,'' Jacqueline said, just a fraction of a second before Charlotte chipped in with, ''The florist.''

Chloe eyed them severely. ''Would you like me to

leave you alone for a few minutes, so that the pair of you can get your stories straight?''

''Oh, stop being such a lawyer!'' her mother said, in that pooh-pooh voice Chloe well knew was designed to throw her off track. ''We haven't committed any crimes that we're aware of. Eat your blueberries. I read somewhere that they're very good for you.''

But her grandmother's next remark left Chloe feeling too sick to the stomach for her to eat so much as a mouthful. ''Just remember, precious, that things don't always turn out the way you expect them to. Life sometimes throws you a curve.''

''You think I don't know that, Gran?'' she said quietly. ''You think I didn't learn that lesson in the most cruel way possible?''

''Of course you did, my sweetheart, and it's not my intention to open up old wounds. All I'm trying to say is that, no matter what might come about, your happiness, your...*choices*...are the most important things in the world to us. We only ever want the very best for you.''

Choices? That was an odd word, surely, especially at a time like this? ''Then you must be thrilled that I chose Baron, because he's the best thing that's happened to me in a very long time.''

''If you say so, Chloe.''

''I do, Gran. So why, I wonder, don't you believe me?''

''Perhaps,'' her mother cut in, ''because you don't seem able to whip up any great enthusiasm for this wedding. To put it bluntly, Chloe, no one would believe you're the bride, the way you're distancing yourself from it all. Why, when you married Nico—!''

"I was twenty-two, and foolishly idealistic."

"You were so eager to become *Signora* Nico Moretti that you practically galloped down the aisle to meet him at the altar." Jacqueline closed her eyes and let out a sentimental sigh. "I remember your veil flying out behind you like a parachute, and the crinoline on your dress swinging like a pendulum. Your joy was so infectious, everyone in the church was smiling by the time you reached his side. They all commented on how radiant you were."

"Nerves will do that to a person."

"You were deeply in love—and so was Nico."

"Not quite deeply enough, as it turned out. Our marriage didn't last."

"It could have," Charlotte said. "It *should* have."

Annoyed, Chloe pushed aside the blueberries. "Is there a reason you're both raking up the past like this? Is it, by chance, your way of telling me you think I'm making a mistake in marrying Baron?"

"Do *you* think you are?" Jacqueline asked.

"No!" she said, a shade too emphatically. "And if you two do, you've left it a bit late in the day to mention it." Beset by her own niggling uncertainty, she glared at the women she loved most in the world. "You're the ones, after all, who insisted on turning a small, quiet wedding into a three-ring circus!"

Jacqueline's face almost crumpled, but at the last minute she regained control of herself. "Because we wanted to show you how much we love you, Chloe. We want so badly for you to move forward with your life and find real happiness again."

"I know," Chloe murmured, ashamed. It wasn't their fault she couldn't let go of the past.

"We hoped marrying Baron would be the key, but you seem so...*indifferent*, somehow—as if marrying him is just another case to deal with. You weren't even going to buy a proper wedding dress until we bullied you into it. As for the gifts people are sending, why, you haven't bothered to open half of them!"

"Because I'm preoccupied with my workload at the moment," she hedged. "Taking all next week off is bad enough, but tack on the month we'll be in the Bahamas after that, and it's asking a lot to expect others in the firm to cover both for me *and* Baron. As for buying a wedding dress, well, it seemed a bit over the top for the second time around, especially given the closet full of clothes I already own."

"Even a quiet second wedding deserves some fanfare," her grandmother observed. "It *is* a special day, after all."

"You're right, of course." Tired of the subject, she directed her next question at Jacqueline. "How many people are we expecting tonight, Mother?"

"About a dozen, only—just family, those in the wedding party, and a few friends. We didn't want to swamp the Prescotts with too many new faces all at once. What time are they flying in from down east?"

"Eleven-twenty, I believe. Baron's going to pick them up and take them to lunch, then leave them to settle in at their hotel and catch an afternoon nap before the party." She pushed back her chair. "Which reminds me, I'd better get going. I promised him we'd sneak away for coffee before he heads out to the airport. We've both been so busy this last few days, we've only seen one another in passing, and it doesn't look as if the coming week's going to be much better.''

''You'll have the rest of your lives together after next Saturday,'' Jacqueline pointed out. ''In the meantime, with all the social engagements we've got planned, you'll be seeing each other pretty much every day, even though you won't be going in to the office.''

This was true, but the fact was, Chloe needed some private time with her fiancé, away from all the pre-wedding hoopla. She needed his steadying influence to soothe her frazzled nerves; his calm, quiet voice to drown out the diabolical whispers of doubt which persisted in creeping up on her. She needed to feel his arms around her, to bask in the warmth of his slow, sweet smile.

That's all it would take for her doubts to evaporate, and bring home the realization of how lucky she was to have found him. How could it be otherwise when he was everything a woman could want in a husband—patient, kind and loyal? And so in tune with her own wishes that it was little short of miraculous.

''Before you give me your answer,'' he'd cautioned, the night he'd proposed, ''I have to reiterate what I've mentioned before. I really do *not* want children, or a house in the suburbs, with a big garden and neighbors who like to get together around the barbecue every Friday evening. I'll be forty in November, and I don't see myself spending weekends mowing lawns or coaching soccer for small boys. You and I are dedicated professionals, Chloe, with both of us putting in long hours Monday through Friday. When we're not working, I want us to be free to concentrate on each other, to be able to lock the front door and take off, without the attendant stress of babies who'll eventually grow up to be…'' He'd shuddered. ''…teenagers. Am I asking for too much?''

"Absolutely not!'' she'd told him, closing the door on memories of how it had been the last time a man had proposed to her. ''We're exactly in tune on the kind of life we want. So yes, I'll marry you, and be proud to call myself Mrs. Baron Prescott—socially, at least.''

"Of course.'' He'd stroked the hair back from her face and regarded her fondly. ''I'd never ask you to give up everything you've worked so hard to achieve. It goes without saying that, professionally, you'll always be Ms. Chloe Matheson, attorney-at-law.''

And that, she'd thought at the time, was more than enough to make her happy. Because Baron was right. The steady stream of desperate women coming to her for help in escaping an unbearable marriage, haunted her. As for the innocent children caught up in such messes, they broke her heart. And Baron, dealing mostly with wills and estates, witnessed sufficient family in-fighting to persuade him that nothing brought out the ugliness in siblings more than the division of a parent's worldly goods. Cocooning their lives around just the two of them made perfect sense.

Only now, with her second wedding day just little more than a week away, did it occur to her that accepting his terms so readily might have had a lot less to do with love than it had with safety—from hurt, disillusionment, loneliness…and always, always, from grief.

* * *

She might have wished for a more scaled-down wedding, but Chloe had to admit that, if a grander affair was in the scheme of things, no one could beat her mother at doing it in style. As a prelude of even greater things to come, the cocktail party was a triumph of understated elegance.

Of course, it didn't hurt any that the balmy evening meant the French doors could stand open, allowing guests to drift from the drawing room to the patio, to admire the sunset gilding the Strait and etching the distant islands in flaming gold. Add an endless supply of the very finest caviar, accompanied by enough excellent champagne to float a battleship, and by the time daylight dwindled to dusk, it was small wonder most people had loosened up a little.

But despite the surface conviviality, Chloe found the party a strain. Baron's parents moved in an elite social circle. His late grandfather had been a member of parliament, his father was a renowned archaeologist, and his mother the retired headmistress of a prestigious private school for girls. Although pleasant enough, there was no hiding the fact that Mrs. Prescott was sizing up not just Chloe, but Jacqueline and Charlotte, as well as the house, to determine if the bride's upbringing had equipped her sufficiently well that she'd fit in as a Prescott wife and daughter-in-law.

"So how did you find the Prescotts?" Jacqueline inquired, closing the front door as the last car drove away.

"Not all warm and fuzzy, if that's what you're asking," Chloe said bluntly. "Frankly, I'm glad they live at the other end of the country. From the way Baron's mother quizzed me about the fact that I'd been married before, I got the impression she considered me soiled goods.''

"I noticed that, too," her grandmother remarked. "She was really rather snooty at first, although she did warm up to us a little, toward the end."

"It was the Waterford chandelier that did it." Jacqueline choked back a laugh. "Myrna Prescott almost swallowed her teeth when she saw it. I think both she and her husband went away quite favorably impressed with our standard of living."

"As they should have!" Charlotte said, still the protective parent even at seventy-six. "They might have an illustrious family tree, but you didn't exactly grow up on the wrong side of the tracks yourself, my love. Tonight's little get-together was a triumph. You really outdid yourself, and you must be exhausted."

"I am a little tired."

"Then I'm taking you to the Inn for dinner. It's been a long time since just the two of us went out." She paused delicately. "Of course, you're welcome to join us, Chloe, if you wish...."

"Oh, absolutely not!" Chloe was quick to answer. "I want nothing more than to kick off my shoes and relax. Go ahead and have a good time. Heaven knows you're both working hard enough putting this wedding together that you deserve a bit of a break."

They didn't bother to put up an argument. In fact, they seemed almost eager to leave her behind. Not that they said as much, of course. Instead, they agreed that she was quite right to take it easy, then the pair of them hurried out to the car and drove off before she could change her mind.

By then, it was well after eight but although darkness had fallen, the heat of the day lingered, leaving the air so soft and warm that, instead of taking a long, luxurious bath, she pulled on an old bathing suit and went down to the pool for a swim.

"Just eight more days to get through, then all this craziness will be over. A week from Sunday, we'll be on our way to the Bahamas," Baron had whispered, when he kissed her good-night. "I can hardly wait, Chloe...."

Slipping into the limpid water, Chloe floated on her back and gazed up at the heavens, willing herself to share his eager anticipation. Next Saturday at this time, they'd have been married nearly five hours. They'd be in the honeymoon suite of the hotel where they planned to spend the night. Chances were, they'd already have made love for the first time.

Would it be wonderful, the way it had been with—?

Her mind snapped shut on the thought, as suddenly and mercilessly as a leg-hold trap. She would not allow Nico to creep in; he had no place in her life anymore.

Just then, a meteor streaked across the velvet sky in a shower of sparks. A lucky sign, according to some. *Make a wish,* they'd say—and she would, if she didn't already have everything any woman could wish for.

Everything, except one thing, that is. And there was no use wishing for that, because it was asking for the impossible. Neither prayers nor superstition could breathe life back into her little son.

Instead, "I wish I could forget," she whispered, tears blurring her vision and turning the blanket of stars into a shimmering arc of rainbows. "I wish it really was possible to start afresh and leave the past behind."

* * *

He picked up his phone on the second ring. *"Sì?"*

"The coast's clear, Nico. Make your move."

"Does she suspect?"

"Not a thing."

He smiled, switched off the phone, and headed out the door.

She hadn't known he'd been watching her all evening as she moved about the garden with her fiancé and his family, the mother fat as a pigeon, the father tall and thin. She'd had no idea that he'd stood at the dormer window in the gardener's lodge and seen how his replacement had slung his arm around her shoulder and nuzzled her hair. How he'd kissed her when he thought no one else was looking—full on the mouth, with the sort of hungry need Nico understood only too well.

Treading stealthily, he followed the brick walk from the lodge to the main house, shrouded in darkness now except for the light shining from her bedroom. Of course, she'd be shocked to see him. Shocked and furious, probably. But his business interests gave him a perfectly valid reason to be in town the same week that she happened to be marrying someone else, and although he could have changed his dates and avoided seeing her again, wild horses hadn't been able to keep him away—especially not after he'd heard her mother's reservations.

"I'm not saying she isn't fond of Baron," Jacqueline had told him. "But there's no real spark there, Nico. She's going through the motions, that's all."

It had been all the encouragement he'd needed to stick with his original plan. "I'll be there by Friday."

"That'll leave you only a week to make her reconsider."

"*Dio,* Jacqueline!" he'd said with a laugh. "It didn't take me more than a day, the first time!"

"But she's different now. She's...wounded."

"We all are," he'd reminded her. "But that's no reason to use another marriage as a refuge from the pain."

"Exactly! Baron's a good man, Nico. He deserves the best, and much though I love her, I'm not sure he'll be getting the best if he marries my daughter. I'm not sure she's able to give him her whole heart."

"I understand."

"Do you? Even though *you* might be the one who ends up being hurt? I'm going only on a mother's instinct here, Nico—a sense that my child is taking the line of least resistance because it's easier to give in than to fight. But I could be wrong. It could be that Chloe really does want this marriage for all the right reasons."

"I've never been afraid of taking risks, you know that. And it seems to me, Jacqueline, that the risk to you is even greater. She might never forgive you for interfering like this."

"It's a chance I have to take."

"There you have it, then. We do what we have to do, and pay whatever price is asked of us. She is worth it, *sì?*"

"Yes."

Which brought him to where he was now, making his way through the shadowed garden, with the advantage of surprise on his side. By catching her with her guard down, he hoped to shock her into revealing a glimpse of that part of her she kept so well hidden from everyone else.

Except that, in the end, he was the one caught off guard, when he stepped out from behind a tall calla lily and activated the motion-detector security lights. Which would have been fine, if she'd been inside the house where he expected her to be. But she wasn't. She was floating on her back in the pool, instead, and before he could dart back behind the concealing foliage, she'd let out a startled squeak and, raising her head, stared straight at him.

Her hair hung around her shoulders in a riot of water-soaked waves, and her legs—those long, glorious legs that used to wrap around him as if they never wanted to let him go…oh, they were a beautiful sight, slicing through the water as she struggled to stay afloat!

There wasn't much point in trying to hide then. So he did the next best thing. He stood there and unashamedly drank in the sight of her.

CHAPTER TWO

CHLOE'S first response at seeing him was one of such utter shock that she swallowed a mouthful of water which went down the wrong way; her second, that either the mixture of light and shadow was playing tricks on her, or she was seeing a ghost. "Tell me you're not real!" she choked, floundering to the side of the pool.

But the figure at the edge of the pool deck looked and sounded frighteningly real. "*Ciao,* Chloe," he said, in that velvet-smooth, sexy Italian voice, and moving forward with his easy, long-legged grace, neither of which appeared to have diminished with time. "Did I startle you?"

"Yes!" she spat, and slapped his hand away when he leaned down and tried to help her out of the water. "Don't you dare touch me!"

He broke into his old, devilishly charming grin, and something turned over inside her in a slow-rolling somersault of awareness. She hadn't felt anything like that in more than four years, and it terrified her. Climbing onto the pool deck, she pushed the wet hair away from her face, flung her towel around her shoulders, and planted her fists on her hips.

"I don't know what you think you're doing here, Nico," she said, with as much controlled dignity as she could manage, given the total upheaval taking place inside her, "but I can assure you, you're not welcome. So unless you wish to spend the night in jail, I suggest you remove yourself from my mother's property immediately.''

''I—'' he began.

''Because,'' she continued, riding roughshod over his attempt to get a word in edgewise, ''if you don't, I'll call the police and have you carted away from here in the paddy wagon.''

He tried to look wounded, but the laughter in his eyes betrayed him. ''You'd do that to me, *cara?*''

''In a heartbeat,'' she informed him stonily. ''And don't call me *cara.*''

''What should I call you, then? *Signora* Moretti?''

''I dropped that name, the day we divorced.''

''You might have dropped the name, but that doesn't change the fact that we were once husband and wife. But I don't suppose you want to be reminded of that, with another man waiting to step into my shoes, in little more than a week's time. What will you call yourself then, my dear?''

''Mrs. Baron Prescott—not that it's any of your business.''

She might as well have saved her breath. Undeterred, he continued his inquisition. ''And you love this Baron person?''

''Why else do you think I'm marrying him?''

He hooked his thumbs in his belt loops and stepped closer. ''What I think isn't the issue here, my lovely Chloe. It's what you think that matters.''

Right at that moment, with him standing close enough that she could detect his faint, alluringly familiar scent, she could barely think at all. *Picture Baron!* she ordered herself. *Concentrate on him!*

But Baron had receded to the farthest reaches of her

mind, dwarfed by the vastly more compelling flesh-and-blood presence of Nico. Helpless to tear her eyes away, Chloe gazed at him.

On the surface, he'd changed little since she'd seen him last. He was still outrageously handsome. Still unmistakably European in the way he wore his clothes, with such sinuous grace that even the unremarkable blue jeans and white polo shirt he had on now assumed the elegance of an Armani suit.

His black hair was as thick as ever, and bore not a trace of gray. His mouth, his teeth, his smile, continued to invite intimacy. As for his darkly beautiful eyes…oh, she couldn't look into his eyes. They reminded her too much of her son's.

"Why do you care what I think or how I feel?" she said bleakly. "I'm not part of your life any longer."

"We had a child together. For that reason alone, there'll always be a connection between us. Nothing and no one will ever break it. You can take a dozen new husbands, *cara mia,* but they'll never succeed in wiping out the memory of the life and the love we once shared."

She pressed her lips together and looked away, desolation sweeping over her in relentless waves. No, she'd never forget, because to do so would mean wiping out the too brief time Luciano had been part of her life, and that she could never do. Memories of him were all she had left. "Do you still miss him, Nico?"

"All the time," he said, knowing without having to ask that she was referring to their baby. "Not a day goes by that I don't think about him, and wish things had turned out differently. He would be four, if he'd lived, and you would not now be contemplating marrying another man, because you'd still be married to me.''

''But he didn't live!'' she cried, all the grief she tried so hard to contain tearing loose inside her like a river bursting its banks. ''And it's your fault that I lost my little boy!''

He jerked his head aside as if she'd slapped him hard across the face, but not so quickly that she didn't see the devastation written there. After a second or two, he turned to look at her again, the suspicion of tears gleaming in his eyes. ''He was my child, too, Chloe.''

Mortified, she clapped a hand to her mouth and whispered, ''Oh, I'm so sorry, Nico! I shouldn't have said that. I know it's not true. But the hurt never really goes away, and seeing you again brings it all back as if it happened just yesterday.'' She huddled more closely into the towel, shivering suddenly despite the mild air. ''What are you really doing here?''

''I always stay here when I come to Canada.'' He shrugged, as if making himself at home in his ex-mother-in-law's house was the most natural thing in the world. ''You might have divorced me, but Jacqueline never did. She has always made me welcome.''

''But why now?'' she pursued, hiding her dismay at his revelation. ''If you knew I was remarrying next week, you must have realized this was not the time for you to show up unannounced.''

''It could not be avoided. When business calls....'' He shrugged and to her shame, she found she couldn't quite drag her gaze away from the easy shift of his broad shoulders under his shirt. ''I must answer, yes?

And since I will be here for at least ten days, Jacqueline invited me to attend your wedding. Such a lovely, gracious lady, your mother!''

With each shocking disclosure, he moved toward her. And every time he did so, Chloe took a step back, desperate to maintain distance from him because she didn't dare think of what might happen if she let him come too close. Bad enough that her body ached with vague yearning, as if it recognized that there'd been a time when he'd brought it to vibrant, thrilling life. *''She did not!''*

''She most certainly did,'' he said, lunging forward without warning and grabbing her around the middle.

His hands almost spanned her waist, his fingers so strong and sure that she hadn't a hope of escaping him. ''One more step and you'd have toppled backward into the pool,'' he murmured, drawing her away from one kind of danger and toward another, far more perilous.

At once panic-stricken and hypnotized, she stammered, ''I don't believe you! Why would she do such a thing?''

''Because ours was the most civilized divorce in the world, so where is the harm in wishing you and this new man well, and showing him he has nothing to fear from me?''

''He already knows that.''

''Then my being here won't disturb him, will it?''

''Not a bit!''

''And what about you, Chloe? Will knowing I'm close by make you less sure of yourself and the plans you've made?''

''Absolutely…not…'' The denial emerged on a sigh, defeated almost before it was uttered, because he was stroking his hands up her ribs, over her shoulders, down her arms, and robbing her of every last ounce of strength. Her legs grew weak as water, her vision clouded, and she felt herself swaying toward him.

He put her from him very firmly. "Then there's no problem. Consider me nothing more than another guest, here to witness your marriage and toast your future happiness. It'd be a shame for me to have come all this way and miss such a grand event. You know how much we blue-collar Italians love a good party."

Throwing cold water in her face would have been less shocking than what he proposed. The strength flowed back into her body, fortified by a dose of righteous indignation. "You are not coming to my wedding, and that's final! I'll see you in hell, first!"

"Darling," he said lazily, "I've already spent enough time there. I doubt anything you can devise to punish me now will ever equal that."

How easily he could seduce her with a touch wasn't the only thing she remembered. He was beyond stubborn, too, once he'd made up his mind about something. "Be reasonable, Nico," she begged, trying to keep the frantic edge out of her voice. "You'll feel awkward…a man alone at a wedding is out of place. People will talk and wonder why you're here. And even if they don't, I can't imagine why you'd want to see me marry someone else."

"Because your happiness is important to me."

"But why do you care? You're not responsible for me anymore."

"I'll always feel responsible, *cara.* You suffered more sorrow with me than any woman should have to bear. If I couldn't be the one to heal you, I want to shake the hand of the man who can.''

She saw the obstinate set to his jaw, the way he planted his feet apart, as though to say, *If you want rid of me, you're going to have to pick me up and remove me by force.*

Trying to disguise the desperation creeping up on her, she said, ''I won't allow this, Nico. You're not going to bully me into letting you stay. I don't want you here, it's as simple as that. Consider yourself uninvited.''

''Can't do that, it wouldn't be polite,'' he replied, all sweet reason. ''Your mother's the one who issued the invitation, and this is her house. Until *she* tells me I'm not welcome, I stay.''

I will kill her! Chloe vowed furiously. *So help me, I will wring my mother's scheming neck, the very first chance I get!*

''We'll see about that,'' she told him. ''Unlike you, my mother can be persuaded to change her mind.''

''Why does my being here make you so nervous, *cara?* Are you afraid I'll embarrass you?'' He indicated his snug-fitting jeans, his blindingly white shirt. ''Do you think I'll show up dressed like this on your big day? That I'm still scratching to make ends meet, and can't afford a decent suit and tie? Because if so, rest easy. I'm respectably rich now.''

''If how much you're worth was that important to me, I'd never have married you in the first place,'' she said scornfully. ''I didn't fall in love with your money.''

He laughed. ''How could you? I didn't have any!'' Then he sobered, and when he spoke next, his voice had grown gentle with nostalgia. "I remember so well the day we met. Do you?"

"Not really."

He looked up at the stars and smiled, as if he and they shared a secret. "It was a Tuesday."

"Thursday," she corrected.

"At a jewelry booth."

"In an antique shop which happened to sell estate jewelry, which isn't quite the same thing."

"*Sì!*" He nodded and adopted the smiling pose of a professor faced with an unusually bright student. The only thing missing was a beard—and so help her, if he'd had one, she'd have pulled it out by the roots! "It was just as you say. I had found a cameo brooch which I planned to give to my sister, Abree, for her birthday."

"I found it first, but you tried to outbid me on it."

"So I did." His smile shifted to her face and bathed it in unsettling warmth. "But in the end, I let you win because why quibble over such a trifling piece, when already you had stolen my heart?"

"Your heart had nothing to do with it! You couldn't meet my offer, and pulled your jeans' pockets inside out to prove it."

But it was the way he'd laughed as he relinquished his claim that had won her over. In the blink of an eye, he made her forget that she'd come to Italy to visit fabled art galleries, to walk the ancient streets and experience history firsthand, in still-living color. Meeting him that day in Verona instantly became the most memorable event in the tour she and Monica embarked on, to celebrate their having graduated *summa cum laude* from university.

"I will concede defeat," he'd said, with irresistible Latin charm, "only if you will let me take you to lunch. I have just enough lire in my pocket to buy us a carafe of wine and a bowl of pasta. Do we have a deal?"

She'd agreed without a moment's hesitation, and was in love with him before they arrived at the *trattoria* he chose, tucked away in a tiny sunlit square which she'd never have discovered on her own. To say he typified an Italian matinee idol would have been to sell him so far short of reality that it was an insult. Nico was the most beautiful, the most gallant, the most beguiling man she'd ever met. It hadn't mattered one iota that he was virtually penniless.

"I recently invested my limited assets in a business on the brink of bankruptcy," he told her cheerfully, over ravioli and a jug of rough red wine.

"Everything?" The future lawyer in her had been appalled. "What if you end up with nothing?"

He'd laughed. "I grew up with nothing, *la mia bella,* and if I die with nothing, it will matter not at all, as long as I squeeze from life every last drop of joy it has to offer. A man must make the most of his time on earth, *sì?"*

She'd realized then how different they were in outlook. He was the kind of man who dared to imagine; to take risks; to act on impulse and live with the consequences. She was nothing like that, and although she admired those qualities in him, they were also what made him dangerous. But that was something she didn't discover until it was much too late.

"Do you still have it?" he asked her now. "That brooch which brought us together?"

"No," she said. "I gave it away at about the same time that I left you. I couldn't bear the reminder of what it represented."

"Did getting rid of it help you to forget?"

"No."

"I'm glad. There was too much that was good between us for it all to be cast into oblivion." He touched her hair. "We were happy for a little while, weren't we, Chloe?"

Oh, yes! Blissfully so, almost from the second she first set eyes on him...until that terrible, terrible night. Perhaps that was why the grief that followed was so hard to bear.

Monica had continued touring the country, but Chloe stayed in Verona, any thought of discovering more of Italy abandoned. In fact, "abandoned" was a very good word to describe the way she'd behaved over the next month.

Within a week, she and Nico were lovers. By the end of the summer, he asked her to marry him and just as well, or she'd have proposed to him.

With a tiny diamond on her finger, she flew home at the beginning of September and flung herself into preparations for a wedding to take place in early October, even though her mother and grandmother voiced reservations at the suddenness of it all.

"What about your career?" they'd wanted to know, and she'd told them, "Nico is my career now."

"How can you be sure?" they'd said. "At least wait until next summer before you marry him, to give yourself time to find out if this really is love, or just a holiday infatuation."

But she was not to be dissuaded, and when Nico

arrived in Vancouver at the end of the month, both her mother and grandmother fell under his spell as swiftly and easily as she had.

"When the right man comes along," Jacqueline had decreed within twenty-four hours of meeting him, "the timing isn't important. You're meant for one another, my darling daughter. I can't think of any other man I'd sooner call son-in-law."

Clearly, nothing that had happened since that day had changed her mother's mind. She still considered Nico family; still thought the sun rose and set on him. Why else would she have jeopardized her only child's future by allowing him to come back on the scene now?

"You don't answer me, Chloe," Nico said, sliding his hand around the back of her neck. "Were we not happy for a little while? Our wedding day, was it not perfect?"

She had to force herself to answer truthfully. It would have been so much easier to dismiss both him and the question, if she could have said "no."

Instead, "Yes," she admitted grudgingly, "though if I'd been in your shoes, I wouldn't have found it so special. None of your family came to see you get married."

"The distance and cost involved made it impossible for them to attend, and in truth, I hardly noticed their absence. *You* were there, beyond beautiful in white satin and lace, and that was enough for me. Indeed, you could have worn sackcloth for all I cared. That you were about to become my wife was the only thing that mattered. I might not have had the means to fly my family here from Italy but, that day, I felt like the richest man on earth. What was money, compared to your promise to remain by my side, through good times and bad, for as long as we both should live?''

The passion in his voice, the drugging seduction of his fingers strumming a love song over the nape of her neck, were making deadly inroads on her self-possession, and she had to put a stop to them before she fell so far under their spell that she ended up in his arms.

''I think your memory is deceiving you,'' she said, trying to wriggle out of his reach. ''Being poor bothered you a very great deal—to the point that making money eventually became your obsession.''

''I needed to provide well for you and our son, Chloe. Do not fault me for that. Before I met you, I'd made myself a promise that I wouldn't marry until I could support a wife and family in some sort of style. But you bewitched me into forgetting all that. I knew the day I met you that you were the woman for me. But I never regretted making that decision. I still do not, even now, even though we ended up so far apart.''

''Perhaps we both wanted too much, too soon. Perhaps what we had was too good to last.''

''Or perhaps we didn't fight hard enough to hold on to it.''

''How do you hold on to a three-and-a-half-month-old baby lying in a casket, in a church graveyard?'' she cried. ''How do you *ever* recover from that?''

''By sharing your grief with the one person in the world who really understands it. But we couldn't do that, could we, Chloe? Instead of turning toward each other, we turned away, and in doing so, lost so much more than our son. We threw away everything else that was good and beautiful between us.''

"Don't you see, we had nothing left? Everything we were, or hoped to be, died with him.''

"If you truly believe that, then you're doing the right thing in marrying your Baron.''

"I do believe it, Nico," she said with hushed vehemence. "I believe it with my whole heart. I can make a fresh start with him because he doesn't threaten my peace of mind. He is…my safe harbor. He won't hurt me.''

"Then no wonder you are finally ready to trade me in for this older model.''

"*Mature* is how I'd describe my fiancé!''

"Ah!" He rolled his eyes. "If only I could have been such a paragon of manly virtues!''

She wrenched herself free of his touch and raced toward the house, stopping at the far end of the pool deck just long enough to hurl a final bit of advice over her shoulder. "Do yourself and everyone else a favor and go home, Nico, because if you have any idea of upsetting my wedding plans, you're wasting your time here. I'm going to marry Baron next Saturday, and nothing you can say or do is going to change my mind.''

Nothing? "We'll see about that, *tesoro*," he murmured softly, remaining in the garden long after she'd disappeared inside the house. "I have seven days in which to prove to you that, whatever you might want to believe, all the passion you think died with our son is still very much alive. And it will be my very great pleasure to reawaken it. I think then that you will be unwilling to settle for *a safe harbor* with this Baron Prescott. I think you'll find he will not be enough for you, after all.''

CHAPTER THREE

Saturday, August 22

ANOTHER perfect summer's day, another breakfast on the sunny patio, and the only storm on the horizon the one brewing between mother and daughter.

"How *could* you?" Chloe exploded, glaring at Jacqueline across the table. "And spare me the injured innocence act. You know perfectly well what I'm talking about. What in heaven's name possessed you to invite Nico to stay here?"

"He always stays here whenever he's in town. I thought you knew that."

"But why *now?*" She shook her head, so baffled she could scarcely string two words together without exploding. "You've spent weeks orchestrating this wedding, Mother. So why, at the last minute, would you go out of your way to turn it into a shambles?"

"Because, in the final analysis, a mother has to do what she thinks best for her child, especially if that child is determined to hide her head in the sand and pretend everything's perfectly lovely, when it would be apparent to a blind man that it's not."

"Are you saying you deliberately encouraged Nico to come here at this time in the hope that he'd ruin things for me?"

"No. I had no idea he'd planned a visit to coincide with your wedding. But when I found out, I couldn't help but think that destiny was stepping in and taking a hand in your future.''

Stunned, Chloe said, ''In other words, you might not have planned it, but you're hoping it will happen anyway?''

''He can't spoil anything unless you allow him to. If you're absolutely sure you're doing the right thing in marrying Baron, you won't let anyone stand in your way. But if, simply by his being here, Nico changes your mind, he'll have saved you and Baron both from making a terrible mistake.''

''He won't change my mind! I know what I'm doing.''

''So you keep saying. But it's not the impression I've been getting lately.''

''Then take another look! I'm twenty-eight years old, Mother, and capable of making my own decisions. I haven't needed you to wipe my nose since my first day in kindergarten, and I don't need you interfering now in something that's absolutely none of your business!''

Unruffled, her mother said, ''You'll always be my business, Chloe, just as you'll always be my daughter, no matter how old you are. And I could not, in all conscience, stand idly by and do nothing when, the closer you get to your wedding day, the more unsettled you become.''

''I am *not* unsettled!''

''Certainly you are. I'd even go so far as to say you're depressed. Now sit down and have a peach.''

She'd sooner eat worms! Clutching the back of her chair in a white-knuckled grip, she asked mournfully,

"Have you considered how Baron will feel when he finds out what you've been up to?"

"One way or the other, I suspect that, in the end, he'll thank me."

Bewildered, Chloe stared at her. "I thought you and Gran liked him."

"We do, darling—enough not to want to see him hurt."

"You've got a funny way of showing it! Inviting my ex-husband to stay here is bad enough, but to suggest he's welcome at the wedding…how am I supposed to explain that to Baron in a way that makes any sort of sense?"

"You're not," her mother said, unperturbed. "If there's any explaining to be done, I'll take care of it."

"Over my dead body!" Chloe dropped down on her chair, exhausted before the day had properly begun. "You've caused enough trouble, Mother! *I'll* speak to Baron. If you really want to do something worthwhile, get rid of Nico, and spare us all a lot of grief."

As if he'd been lurking in the bushes waiting for the right moment to make an entrance, Nico suddenly strolled around the corner of the house. "Did I hear someone mention my name?"

Chloe scowled at him, but her mother and grandmother, their faces wreathed in welcoming smiles, chorused, "Good *morning, Nico!"

"Did you sleep well?" Charlotte inquired solicitously.

"Like a baby, *Nonna!"* he replied, bending to kiss her cheek. "You're looking wonderful, as usual, and younger than ever."

Jacqueline, meanwhile, poured him a cup of coffee.

"Here you are, dear. Strong and black, just the way you like it."

He dropped a kiss on her cheek, too. "*Grazie,* Jacqueline! As always, you know exactly how to make me feel at home."

Chloe, though, refused to acknowledge him, and stared instead at the coffee cooling in her own cup. Totally unfazed by her chilly reception, he took a seat next to her. "*Buon giorno, bella! Come sta?*"

"No happier to see you today than I was last night," she informed him bluntly. "Don't make yourself too comfortable in the lodge, Nico. You won't be staying there, after all."

"No?" She didn't need to look at him to sense his smile. She could feel its warmth stealing over her face like a second sun. "I am to take over my usual room here, in the main house?"

"We don't have space for you there, either. If you're determined to hang around, you'll have to move to a hotel, and it won't be the Trillium Inn, because it's booked up with people whom Baron and I *want* to have at our wedding. So you'll be forced to look at something downtown."

"Chloe," her mother interposed gently, "why do you care where Nico sleeps, as long as it isn't in your bed, with you?"

The mere suggestion of such a possibility sent such a stab of forbidden pleasure coursing through her body that Chloe was left blushing and breathless. And of course, *he* noticed! Leaning so close that his shoulder brushed hers, he murmured, "Don't worry, *cara.* It will happen only when you give the word."

"Dream on!" she choked indignantly.

Trying to avert another storm, Jacqueline quickly changed the subject. "So sorry we couldn't welcome you properly last night, Nico, but as I mentioned when you phoned during your layover in Toronto, we were entertaining Baron's parents whom we met for the first time. I'm sure you understand how awkward it would have been to explain your presence to them, had we included you in the party."

"Do not be concerned," he practically crooned, so full of beaming good cheer that Chloe came perilously close to smacking him. "I found the key to the lodge exactly where you said it would be, and was comfortably settled in by what…?" He lifted his shoulders in one of his supremely careless shrugs. "Six o'clock? Half past?"

"And you have everything you need?"

"But yes! More than enough. The bed…." Another shrug, this time accompanied by an expansive forefinger-to-thumb gesture of approval. "*Molto comodo! Very comfortable!*" He angled a sly glance at Chloe. "But much too big for just one person."

"Don't give me that look," she informed him tartly. "It'll be a cold day in hell before I jump into any bed with you again!"

"Did I ask that you do so, *cara?*"

"No, but it's what you're thinking!"

"And since when am I not allowed to dream?"

"Since you found out I'm engaged to another man." She drew in an irate breath. "I won't tolerate your causing trouble for Baron and me, Nico. Contrary to the impression my mother might have given you, we thought long and hard before we decided to get married, and we're not about to let you or anyone else put an eleventh-hour dent in our plans.''

''But, darling, how could I if, as you claim, you're meant for one another?''

Dar-ling, he said, endowing both syllables with such husky, continental emphasis that her spine tingled. She tossed down her napkin and abruptly rose from her seat. ''You can't, and you won't get a chance to try. If it were up to me, I'd have you tossed out of here on your ear, but since it's not, I'll make sure we cross paths as little as possible. And on those occasions when our being in the same place at the same time is unavoidable, I shall ignore you. And now, if you'll excuse me, I have things to do.'' Sparing her mother but a passing glance, she dropped a kiss on Charlotte's head. ''I'll see you later, Gran.''

''You're going out?'' Jacqueline sounded surprised, and more than a little disappointed.

''Yes. Baron and I are doing the tourist bit with his family today.''

''So early? It's only just after nine. What's the big rush?''

''He's picking me up at half past, and I'm not quite finished getting ready.''

''Oh, sit down and finish your breakfast!'' her mother declared impatiently. ''You look perfectly fine as you are.''

Nico glanced up from the brioche he was dissecting and swept a critical eye over Chloe's gray linen dress. ''No, she doesn't. She needs to wear something more attractive.''

''Oh, really?'' Chloe fixed him in an affronted glare. ''And exactly what's wrong with what I have on?''

"It is dull and does not suit you." He waved his butter spreader dismissively. "It has no style, no pizzazz. It makes you look like a prison matron. I do not like it."

"How odd!" she cooed, masking her outrage with a heavy dose of sarcasm. "You must have mistaken me for someone who *cares* about your likes or dislikes!"

She swept away then, chased by his taunting laughter and the echo of his words. They followed her inside the house and up the stairs to her bedroom. ...*No style, no pizzazz... I do not like it...like it...like it....*

"Much he knows!" she muttered scornfully. "He wouldn't recognize style if it jumped up and bit him in the face!"

But when she crossed to the full-length mirror in the corner, what she saw staring back at her was not a sleekly elegant woman wearing a designer creation the color of sea mist, but a drab, featureless individual in a drab, featureless dress. Her hair, newly styled just the day before, hung around her face in a limp brown mass, looking as defeated as she felt at that moment. Her eyes, which Nico once had compared to sparkling sapphires, reflected the emptiness in her soul, their dark blue irises lifeless. Even her skin appeared faded.

When had it happened? Since yesterday? Or had the change been more subtle, and crept up a little at a time, as her wedding day grew closer?

"Ah!" Furious with Nico for making her doubt herself, and with herself for letting him get away with it, she rushed into the bathroom. Smoothed blusher on her cheeks, and a trace of lilac shadow over her eyelids. Brushed a mascara wand over her lashes, and applied rosy lip gloss to her mouth. Dabbed a little perfume behind her knees and in the crook of her elbows. Then, snatching up a brush, she raked it through her hair until her scalp burned.

"There!" she muttered, watching as her hair bounced gently into place. "Now tell me I look like a prison matron!"

But how she looked wasn't the issue. It was that Nico's opinion could carry such weight after all this time. What kind of fool was she, that she'd let him derail her so easily?

Taking a deep, calming breath, she returned to the bedroom and, refusing to listen to the little voice telling her to change into something else, she hunted through her jewelry case for an item to accessorize her dress.

Not the plain gold locket and chain, she decided: it had no *style!* And definitely not the dignified pearls; they lacked *pizzazz!* But the long string of turquoise baroque beads, with matching dangling earrings? Now there was drama and color enough to turn a prison uniform into haute couture, and let anyone try to tell her differently!

When she came back downstairs, the front door stood open. "So you travel over here fairly frequently, then?" she heard Baron say as she reached the bottom step, and realized with utter horror that he'd arrived already and was speaking to Nico.

"*Sì.* At least three or four times a year."

That often? She'd had no idea! Had thought, from her mother's passing references, that he'd visited only once or twice since the divorce.

"Business must be good, then."

"I do not complain. And with you, business is also good?"

"No complaints here, either. I keep busy, but always find time to put in a round or two of golf each week. Do you play?"

"Not as often as I'd like, but I enjoy it when I have the chance."

"Maybe we can work in a game while you're here."

Time to step in and effect a little damage control, Chloe decided, and practically flew the last several yards from the foot of the stairs to the front door. "I can't see that happening, with everything else going on," she said breezily, sweeping past Nico as if he were just another planter of petunias, and pressing a kiss on Baron. "Hi, sweetheart. I didn't hear the car arrive, or I'd have been down sooner."

"I got here only a couple of minutes ago. Just long enough to say hello to your mother and meet Nico." He caught her hand. "You look beautiful, Chloe. But then, you always do."

"Thanks." She squeezed his fingers, so grateful for the understanding she read in his smile that she could have wept. He knew her so well; better than anyone else ever had. She didn't need to tell him how distraught she was. His calm blue eyes saw it all. "We should be on our way, don't you think? Your family will be waiting."

"Yes." He paused with his hand on her elbow and nodded amiably at Nico. "Nice meeting you. We'll see each other again, I'm sure."

"But certainly," Nico returned, his gaze resting fleetingly on Chloe before focusing on Baron. "*Ciao!* Enjoy your day."

She waited just long enough for the car doors to slam closed before starting to explain. "I didn't invite him," she began. "Honestly, Baron, I had no idea he was coming, or I'd have put a stop to it. I don't know what my mother was thinking about."

Baron reached over and briefly covered her hand. "Honey, it's okay. I don't mind that he's here."

"You don't?" Thunderstruck, she stared at him. "He's my ex-husband, for heaven's sake!"

"He's also a family friend, and strikes me as a decent enough guy. His timing might be a bit off, but I can handle it, if you can."

That was the trouble in a nutshell; she wasn't sure she could. Wasn't sure of anything anymore, if truth be told. "What will your parents think?"

"That he's just another guest, unless you choose to tell them differently. They don't have to know you were once married to him. It's none of their business."

"He thinks he's coming to the wedding, Baron!"

"Where's the harm in that? I hardly expect he's going to fling himself down on the ground and throw a tantrum in the middle of the ceremony. He doesn't strike me as the type. In fact, if he still harbors any romantic affection for you, seeing you marry me might be the one thing to give him closure."

More confounded by the second, Chloe shook her head. "You amaze me! If it were your ex-wife we'd just left standing on the doorstep, I can tell you I wouldn't be taking it nearly this well."

"Why not? Don't you trust me to know who it is I want to be with?"

"You know that I do."

"Well, the same goes for me. Unless you tell me

differently, I'm assuming nothing's changed between us." He patted her hand again. "I know you well enough to recognize that you don't have a dishonest bone in your body, Chloe. You'd never lie about your feelings."

He was trying very hard to make her feel better, she realized. What he couldn't begin to guess was that, with his every word, she felt worse.

Nico spent the day in business meetings in the city, returning to the house just as dusk fell.

"Come join us for dinner," Jacqueline said, intercepting him as he left his rental car and was about to head down the brick path to the lodge. "It'll be just the three of us. Chloe phoned to say she was dining downtown with Baron's family, and won't be home until later."

Not sure if he was disappointed or relieved by the news, he allowed himself to be persuaded. Seeing Chloe again had unraveled him more than he cared to admit. They'd been divorced for more than four years; time enough for both of them to move forward along separate paths. But just as she couldn't come to terms with the death of their son, so he, Nico realized, couldn't accept the idea of some other man replacing him in her life.

Coming upon her in the pool last night had shaken him to the core. He hadn't been prepared to find her so scantily clad that it required no imagination at all to picture her naked.

Ludicrous though it sounded, loss and grief had made her lovelier, stripping her down to a finely sculpted version of the sweetly rounded girl he'd married. Her skin was stretched more tightly over her bones, lending her face an almost ethereal beauty. No one looking at her would guess she'd given birth to a three-kilo baby boy. Her waist and hips were trim, her belly flat, her breasts small and firm, her long, luscious legs unblemished.

"You left so quickly this morning that I didn't get the chance to ask you then," Jacqueline said, the very second they sat down at the table, "but there's nothing stopping us from talking now. So, how do you find her?"

He laughed. His former mother-in-law had always been one to get straight to the point. "Is it possible we're talking about Chloe?" he teased.

"Well, of course! Who else?"

Aware that both mother and grandmother were eyeing him expectantly, he chose his reply with care. "I sense it would not take much to break her."

"So you see it, too!" Jacqueline leaned back in her chair and nodded with satisfaction. "Oh, we're so glad you're here, Nico! You're the one person who might be able to talk some sense into her."

"Or I could be the one to push her into this marriage you feel will be such a mistake. You saw how she was with me this morning. As far as she is concerned, I'm very much a part of her past, and have no place in her present. What makes you think she will listen to anything I say? And perhaps more to the point, do I have the right to say anything at all?"

"I believe you do," Charlotte said in her quiet, thoughtful way, "because I also believe that in her heart, Chloe still loves you. But she can't get past the hurt, and it blinds her to her true feelings. Instead, she's hiding from them, and using Baron to do it.''

"What about you, Nico?" Jacqueline asked, observing him closely. "Do you still love Chloe?"

Did he? Was it love that had sent his heart slamming against his ribs, and left his groin aching painfully, when he'd seen her last night? Or just the normal reaction of any red-blooded man to the sight of a beautiful woman? "We've been apart a long time, Jacqueline. We don't know each other anymore. We've both changed."

"But you care about her?"

"She was the mother of my child. I'll always care."

"Sufficiently to see if there's enough left of what you once had, to build something new?"

Unwilling to let them see the doubt in his eyes, he pushed away from the table and paced to the long windows overlooking the Strait. Had he and Chloe *ever* had enough to make marriage work, if they came apart at the seams the first time something went wrong?

Until that dreadful night, they'd thought they were immune to the woes that afflicted other couples. Had laughed at the idea that anything could ever tarnish their love. Yet in the space of a few minutes, their entire world had crumbled, and only after the dust settled had he realized their marriage lay in ruins because of it....

He'd come home late in the afternoon, to the house they'd rented just before Luciano was born because it had a little alcove off the only bedroom that would serve as a nursery, and a sunny garden where the baby could take his afternoon naps.

He'd burst through the front door, full of excitement. At last, one of his investments had paid off. For the first time, he'd seen a light at the end of the long tunnel of poverty which had marked his childhood and dogged him as a man.

"Put on that dress I like so much, the yellow one, with the daisies all over it," he'd told Chloe, swinging her off her feet in a dizzying circle. "I'm taking you out to dinner, to somewhere fancy, for a change! Tonight, we have something to celebrate!"

"We can't go out," she'd said, laughing down at him. "We're parents now. We have a baby to think about."

"We'll get a sitter—Erstilia, from next door. She's said often enough that she'd be happy to look after Luciano."

Chloe had been aghast. "But we've never left him with anyone else, not even your mother! He's only fourteen weeks old, Nico. What if he needs me?"

"We'll have our phone with us. If there's a problem, we'll come home right away. And Erstilia's twenty— a responsible young woman, who could use a few extra lire to help with her university education."

He'd lowered Chloe to the ground, holding her so close that he felt every inch of her lithe and lovely body sliding against his on the way down. By the time her toes touched the floor, he was hard and wanting, and she…she'd looked up at him, her eyes clouding in that way they did when the passion began to run riot through her veins.

"Come with me," he'd whispered, talking about the restaurant, but meaning the other thing, too; the wild, unfettered loving that they did so well.

She'd sighed, her protest dying, and moved her legs apart so that he could run his hands up under her skirt, pull down her panties, and touch her in exactly the right place to make her whimper and shudder and beg. Then there, against the whitewashed wall just inside the front door, he'd taken her. Swiftly, urgently, with all the raging hunger of a man bewitched by his woman. Felt her contract around him, felt himself surge and explode.

"I love you, Nico," she'd sobbed, burying her face against his neck. She often cried when she came.

"And I adore you, *tesoro*," he'd replied, holding her close. "You are my life."

Luciano had started to wail then, as though he knew he was being left out. They'd drawn apart, smiling, and gone together to soothe him.

"I wouldn't feel right, leaving him," she'd said, leaning over the crib. "He's still so young."

But Nico had coaxed and wheedled until at last, reluctantly, she'd agreed they'd go out to dinner—but *only if* he'd let her wait until Luciano was asleep. *Only if* Erstilia was comfortable about being left with him. *Only if* they didn't stay out too long.

"What is this?" he'd asked, scowling in mock anger. "Am I now number two in your life, that my time with you is rationed to a few short hours?"

"You're my husband," she'd replied softly, "but he is my son and he depends on me to take care of him. Don't make me feel guilty about that."

"Don't make me feel selfish for wanting you to myself, for a change." He brushed his hand down her face and cupped her jaw. "Do you realize we haven't gone out together once in the last three and a half months, unless Luciano's been with us?''

She'd looked at him searchingly, nibbling the corner of her lip the whole time. ''All right, you win,'' she'd said at last. ''We'll go to dinner, just you and me.''

And they had, to one of Verona's finest *ristorante,* in the picturesque Ancient town neighborhood. Overriding her protests, he'd ordered an expensive bottle of wine, a meal fit for a queen and her consort, and laughed when she insisted on keeping the phone beside her on the table so that she'd be sure to hear it, if it rang.

''There's no rush, *cara mia,*'' he'd insisted, when she'd suggested they skip dessert and head home. ''You know Luciano will sleep a good eight hours. We'll be back long before he needs to be fed again.''

''It doesn't feel right to be away from him,'' she'd said.

''He doesn't even know we're gone,'' he'd replied, unable to curb the impatience creeping through his voice. ''*Per carita,* Chloe, I begin to think you don't even know I exist!''

The call that changed their lives forever came at precisely twenty-one minutes after eleven. She'd snatched up the phone on the first ring, and he'd known at once that something had gone terribly wrong. The blood had drained from her face, leaving her white as chalk. And her eyes…dear God, they were the eyes of a woman staring straight into the jaws of hell.

''No!'' she had said, quietly at first. And then over and over again, more loudly, until at last she was screaming the word, and people had come running from all over the restaurant to find out what had happened.

He'd tried to take the phone from her, but she clutched it so tightly that, in the end, he'd had to wrench it from her by force. "I can't wake him up," he heard Erstilia saying, her voice high and terrified. "Please, *Signora* Moretti, come home quickly. He will not open his eyes."

"Call for an ambulance," he barked, suddenly so short of breath that he could barely get out the words. "We'll be home in fifteen minutes."

They were too late. No sooner had they got to say "hello" to their son, than it was time to say "goodbye."

Sudden Infant Death Syndrome, the doctors told them; something no one could have foreseen. It was just one of those things, one of those cruel tricks of fate. No one knew why. No one was to blame.

But Chloe didn't believe them. She blamed him.

He hadn't been able to comfort her. *Dio,* he hadn't known how to comfort himself! The darkness had grown blacker, thicker, until he couldn't move away from it. Couldn't find his way back to the light. It took months…years, before he could look life in the eye again.

By then, he wasn't the same man he'd once been. He lost more than his son, that night. He lost his wife, too, and the best part of himself with her….

He turned away from the windows to confront the two women watching him with such hope in their eyes…such trust. "You're asking the wrong person," he said. "You're looking for a miracle, and that's something only God can grant."

Charlotte sank back in her chair, disappointed acceptance written on her face. But Jacqueline left the table and came to where he stood. "And God helps those who help themselves, Nico!" she said forcefully. "So I ask you again. Do you at least care enough for my daughter to make her stop and look clearly into her own heart, before she walks down the aisle a second time and marries a good man who, through no fault of his own, happens also to be the wrong man?"

Torn between his own selfish needs, and the common decency one man extends to another when a woman is involved, he drew in a breath so deep, he thought his ribs would crack.

Seeing his indecision, Jacqueline struck without mercy at his most vulnerable point. "If you won't do it for yourself or Chloe, Nico, do it for your son. Make Luciano's short time with us amount to more than a memorial to misery and grief. Make it a monument to the healing power of the love he brought into all our lives. He deserves better than to be remembered only for the tears."

CHAPTER FOUR

Sunday, August 23

GIVING up her west-end apartment at the end of July had been a big mistake, Chloe decided. It left her with no place in which to seek refuge; no place to escape the curiosity and gossip Nico's presence aroused. Because keeping his connection to her secret was impossible, something which became glaringly apparent that morning, when her godparents, Phyllis and Steve Stonehouse, who weren't expected until the Monday, showed up a day early.

At Jacqueline's request, Nico was on the patio, busy taking apart the barbecue, when they arrived, "Because," as her mother explained, "the left burner isn't working and I want to cook a salmon on it tonight."

"Well, I never!" Phyllis exclaimed, immediately recognizing him, and hugging him even though his hands were grimy and he had soot smears all down the front of his T-shirt. "Imagine seeing you, of all people! Are you here for the wedding?"

"Only by accident," he replied, favoring her with a grin that would have put a floodlight to shame. "It's coincidence that I happen to be here the same week that Chloe's getting married again."

Practically swooning with pleasure, Phyllis said, "Well, it's lovely to see you, whatever the reason!

And it's *wonderful* that you and Chloe have remained such good friends, even though you're divorced.''

Taking immediate advantage of her godmother's misconception, he'd slipped his arm around Chloe's shoulders and squeezed her fondly. ''I'll always want what's best for Chloe,'' he'd announced magnanimously.

What a liar! If he really had her best interests at heart, he'd have made himself scarce. Taken off for New Guinea, or some other far-flung port of call. But no, he was in her face every time she turned around, watching her every move, and smiling an enigmatic little smile the whole time, as if he nursed some hilarious secret.

After lunch—to which Nico was invited, though why he couldn't make his own meals in the lodge kitchen, was beyond her understanding—Chloe shut herself in the library, on the pretext of sorting through the wedding gifts still waiting to be opened, and writing notes of thanks. But concentrating was difficult, with the low murmur of Nico's voice drifting through the open French doors every other minute.

''Don't be ridiculous!'' her mother had scoffed, when he'd made diffident noises about spending the afternoon in his quarters because he didn't want to intrude on family time. ''It's too nice a day to be indoors. Get your swimming trunks, and join us by the pool. And if you really feel you have to earn your keep, you can man the barbecue later on. Whenever I use it, I more often than not end up setting fire to whatever I'm cooking.''

So there he was, sprawled out on a chaise, basking in sun and approval, and charming the socks off everyone. Meanwhile, Chloe, who had a *right* to be outside, hid in the library and tried not to give in to the urge to sneak a peek at him from between the slats of the blinds on the door.

Why bother? She knew what he looked like, wearing next to nothing. Too darn sexy for his own good— or hers! Which no doubt explained why she couldn't keep her mind on the task at hand.

"What am I trying to prove here anyway?" she muttered, tearing up another ruined envelope in disgust, and adding it to the pile of crumpled paper in the waste basket. "And why in the world am I ostracizing myself from relatives whose company I seldom get the chance to enjoy, and acting as if I don't belong, when *he's* the interloper?"

Because you're afraid of how he makes you feel, Chloe, the brutal, go-for-the-jugular lawyer in her replied. *If, as you claim, you're sure Baron's the man you want, you'd be out there enjoying the afternoon with the rest of your family, regardless of who else happened to be there, not hiding from temptation in here.*

"I'm not afraid," she informed the rows of crystal and sterling and bone china gifts, lined up accusingly on the big library table. "And I'm not tempted!"

No? her alter ego snorted. *You could have fooled me!*

Outside, a chair scraped over the patio paving stones, and Nico's voice, so loaded with the flavor of Italy that she could practically smell the medieval streets of Verona, floated on the air. "*Scusi, per favor, signore e signor.* Much though I'm enjoying your company, there's a business call I must make."

"Use the phone in the library," her mother was quick to offer. "Chloe's in there, but I'm sure she won't mind being disturbed."

Go ahead and do your worst, Mom! Chloe thought sourly, making tracks for the door to the hall before he could act on the suggestion.

But he had other ideas. "*Grazie,* Jacqueline," she heard him reply, "but I need my notes which are in my briefcase. Better, I think, that I phone from the lodge."

"Well, all right. Just don't forget we're counting on you to take charge of the barbecue, later on."

"It will be my pleasure."

And mine, Chloe decided, scuttling upstairs to change into the sleek black one-piece bathing suit she'd been saving for her honeymoon, *to establish my rightful place in this cozy little family gathering, while you're gone.*

When he came back some thirty minutes later, she was ensconced in the chaise he'd previously occupied, with a towel draped ever so casually over her lap, sipping iced tea and giving a very good impression of utter indifference to his return.

"So," he murmured, dropping down beside her, "you were waiting for me to leave before you came out to enjoy the afternoon?"

She lowered her glass, and swung her head toward him, eyes wide with feigned astonishment. "*You* had nothing to do with it."

"But you hoped I would stay away." There it was, the know-it-all smile.

"Believe it or not, Nico," she retorted scathingly,

''you play no part in any decision I make. I was busy earlier. Now I'm not. It's as simple as that.''

''Ah, yes.'' He shrugged off her lie with the same disregard that he rid himself of his short-sleeved white shirt, leaned back on one hand, and stretched his long, powerful legs out in front of him. ''Weddings can consume a person to the exclusion of all else, can they not?''

Unfortunately, in her case, *not.* At that moment, all her attention was fastened on him, despite her best efforts to keep her eyes averted. But the sight of Nico Moretti in navy swimming trunks, lazing like some great tawny cat sunning itself on the warm paving stones, was not a sight any woman in her right mind could ignore easily.

He'd said he had money now, and judging by the expensive rental car he was driving, the very classy gold watch he'd left lying on the patio table, the sunglasses he toyed with in his free hand, and the fine quality cotton shirt he so carelessly cast aside, she supposed it must be true. Yet his body retained the toughness of a man used to hard physical labor. No soft middle or overhanging waistline for him; he was all lean, iron-hard muscle, with arms as strong as ropes and shoulders wide enough to fill the average doorway.

I'm afraid I'll crush you, he'd sometimes say when they were making love, and he'd lift her on top of him, and settle her astride his hips, fitting himself so deeply inside her that she could almost taste him. *That's better,* he'd murmur huskily, cupping her breasts. *I can touch you…watch you…cosi bella….*

He had wonderful eyes; lover's eyes, dark and long lashed. With one meaningful glance, he could make her stomach turn over, her heart take flight, and leave her damp and aching for him.

Aware that his gaze was fixed on her now, that memory had left her nipples hard as pebbles and her skin flushed, she swallowed to relieve her parched throat, and said, "Please excuse me. The sun's a bit more than I can take."

Then, schooling herself not to scuttle away like a frightened mouse, she threw off her towel, and strolled as nonchalantly as she could manage along the deck to the deep end of the pool.

Leaping to his feet, he joined her, and making hardly a ripple, dived cleanly into the water. "Come join me," he invited, surfacing with his hair plastered to his skull and his lashes clumped together in glistening black triangles.

"No, thanks!"

She shied away from the edge, but not soon enough. His hand shot out and fastened around her ankle.

"But if, as you already admitted, the sun is too much for you, why such reluctance? Surely there is no sin in two people sharing such a big pool, as long as they remain in sight of their three chaperones?" His voice, already low and hypnotic, fell to a near whisper. "So what is it that you're really afraid of, *tesoro?*"

"That I might not be able to resist the urge to drown you."

The way he laughed tore at her heartstrings. There'd been a time when they laughed together so often. In public, sometimes, over silly things, but so infectiously that people hearing and seeing them would shake their heads and smile. And sometimes in private, in the quiet intimate way of a couple so deeply in love that all it took to make them happy was being with each other.

"I'll take my chances," he said now, and jerked at her ankle so suddenly that she toppled into the water almost on top of him.

They went under together in a tangle of arms and legs. Of tough masculine muscle and soft feminine curves colliding, then floating apart again. Of hands sliding and clutching at body parts they hadn't touched in years. Of such primal physical contact that Chloe's eyes flew open in shock, and she saw that he had his eyes open, too, and the fire in their depths was such that no amount of water could have quenched it.

Deliberately, he pulled her toward him again, his movements slow and graceful. She drifted close, flotsam caught in a tide too powerful to withstand. Felt herself bump gently against him a second time, limb to limb, hip to hip, shoulder to shoulder. Felt his leg slide between hers, his hands skim past her ribs to cushion her bottom and pull her intimately against him. Against the erection he made no effort to disguise.

Her lungs were burning, her heart thudding. She shook her head, pointed up to where the blue sky shimmered high beyond the water, and pushed against his chest. He nodded understanding, touched his mouth briefly to hers and, with a powerful kick, sent them both shooting to the surface.

"Were *you* trying to drown *me?*" she gasped, when she could draw breath enough to speak.

"No," he murmured ambiguously, his hands circling her waist, his thighs nudging at hers, and his gaze never wavering. "I was trying to save you."

"I don't know what that's supposed to mean!"

"Don't you?" he purred, his eyes stripping her to the soul.

"Chloe? Are you all right?" Another man's voice, horrifyingly familiar, cut through the moment, and Baron, his dear, dear face creased with concern, came running along the deck to where she and Nico bobbed like corks near the diving board. Worse yet, his parents, their expressions variously painted in shades of perplexity and disapproval, observed the entire scene from the patio.

Wishing she *had* drowned, Chloe kicked herself free of Nico's hold and grasped the hand Baron extended to haul her onto the deck. "I'm fine," she said, praying he'd attribute her flush to a coughing fit, and not the guilt which was the real cause. "I just...tripped into the pool and..."

"Swallowcd too much water?" He smiled, and tucked a strand of wet hair behind her ear.

"Um...yes."

"Good thing you didn't hit your head on the diving board when you took a tumble."

Pity she didn't! At least if she'd knocked herself out cold, there'd have been some excuse for being found languishing in Nico's arms, and her future mother-in-law might now be regarding her with a smidgen of sympathy, instead of outright suspicion.

"What are you doing here, Baron?" Chloe asked, turning her back on the pool and its lone occupant. "I thought we weren't supposed to get together until Tuesday, at the town house."

"Well, that's the reason we stopped by, honey. I'm hoping you'll let me beg off going with you to meet the landscape architect. You've got a much better eye for design than I have, anyway, and I thought, since we're booked pretty solid from Wednesday on, that I'd take my folks up to Whistler tomorrow, for a couple of days. It's the only chance they'll get to see the area. They're flying home again right after the wedding.''

"Oh…well, of course. Do that.''

"You're sure you don't mind being left behind?''

What, two days when she didn't have to deal with his overbearing mother, whose expression grew blacker by the second? "Not in the least! Go, and have a good time,'' Chloe said, almost as dismayed by her relief as she was to notice that Nico had swum the length of the pool, toweled himself off, and was in the process of being introduced to Baron's family by her godmother.

Phyllis, bless her heart, didn't subscribe to the theory that less was more; in her view, you could never have too much "more.'' And given the astounded disbelief with which Mother Prescott was regarding Nico, it was pretty obvious that she was being regaled with a whole lot "more'' than she cared to hear.

"Yes, Chloe's *first* husband,'' Phyllis confirmed, as Chloe and Baron joined the group. "He lives in Italy, but he comes over on business once in a while, and always stays here, I'm told. Even though they're divorced, he's still part of the family. Quite an unusual arrangement, wouldn't you say?''

"Quite!'' Mrs. Prescott replied frostily. "Baron's ex-wife is certainly not welcome in my home. I wouldn't dream of entertaining her.'' She turned a glacial eye Chloe's way. "Hello, Chloe. I gather we should have phoned before we dropped in. We obviously caught you unprepared.''

"Not at all, Mrs. Prescott,'' Chloe replied, meeting her glance head-on. "You're welcome anytime, as I'm sure my mother's already told you.''

"Exactly,'' Jacqueline said. "In fact, why don't the three of you stay and have dinner with us? Nico's going to barbecue a salmon, and there's plenty to go around.''

"He *cooks?*'' Mrs. Prescott regarded Nico with the kind of acute disfavor anyone else might have reserved for a scrial killer. "I hope you aren't expecting *my* son to don an apron, once he becomes your husband, Chloe? I've always considered it the woman's job to prepare the meals.''

Clearly aiming to keep the peace at any price, Baron jumped in before Chloe could dish up an answer to that one. "Times are different now, Mother,'' he pointed out. "I daresay Chloe and I will share the household chores. Don't forget she plans to continue working at the law firm after we're married.''

"When I became a wife, I managed to pursue a career *and* cater to your father's needs,'' Myrna Prescott declared loftily. "I've no doubt that's one reason our marriage has lasted.''

Charlotte, who until that moment had been content to listen without comment, said mildly, "I rather think there's more to making a marriage work than who wears the apron. Chloe's grandfather served me coffee in bed every morning until the day he died—and we were very happy together for over forty-five years.''

"Which just goes to prove there's no right or wrong way to go about things,'' Jacqueline said, and gestured to the comfortable chairs scattered around the patio. "Have a seat, everyone, and I'll bring out a little refreshment. Chloe, will you come and help?"

"Of course." She nodded at the Prescotts. "Excuse me, please. I'll be right back."

"Well!" her mother exclaimed, the moment they were safely out of earshot in the kitchen. "If you didn't know before what's expected of a Prescott wife, I guess you do now!"

Beleaguered on every front, Chloe wilted in despair against the counter. "This whole wedding week's turning into a nightmare that never ends, Mom! First, Nico and now Baron's mother! What's next, I wonder?"

"Marriage, and spending the rest of your life with Baron," Jacqueline said somberly, removing plastic wrap from a tray of appetizers she took from the refrigerator, and turning on the oven. "And you do keep insisting how much you're looking forward to that. Or are you ready to admit you're having second thoughts on the matter?"

Chloe buried her face in her hands, caught in the sense of time running out, of impending doom, much like the opening scenes of a movie in which the camera switches from a car racing along a darkened road to a train speeding along the tracks. Without a word being said, people watching know instinctively that, sooner or later, disaster will hit, and all they can do is sit there helplessly, with the tension tightening like an unforgiving screw, until their nerves are ready to snap.

"Don't keep asking me that," she said brokenly. "I feel as if I don't know anything, anymore! My head tells me I'm doing the right thing, but..."

"Your heart tells you differently?" Her mother's

arms came around her. "Maybe you should listen to it, darling."

She wiped a hand across her eyes and broke away. "The last time I did that, it ended up getting broken. I swore then that I'd never let anyone put me through that kind of agony again."

"You can't control everything life throws at you, Chloe. Part of being adult means coming to terms with what fate hands out, and another part means having the guts to admit when you've made a mistake. If you're not ready to get married, just say so. It's not too late to call off the wedding, or even just postpone it. It won't *be* too late until you've said 'I do.'"

"Have you any idea what you're suggesting? Half the guests who live across country are already on their way here. There's enough stuff in the library to open a gift store. Baron and I have bought a town house. We've ordered furniture and rugs and window blinds." She stopped just long enough to draw an overwrought breath, then rushed on, "There's a five-tier cake being decorated, even as we speak, and over a hundred Cornish game hens had their necks wrung and their feathers plucked, to provide the main course at the reception!"

"So?" Jacqueline calmly popped the tray in the oven and began setting out wineglasses and napkins.

"So it's not just about me, Mom!" she almost screeched.

Her mother stopped what she was doing and fixed her in a very direct look. "Is it about Nico?"

Chloe turned to the window, unable to meet Jacqueline's gaze. Outside, her godparents were doing their best to keep Baron's mother and father entertained, which was surely a lost cause. Baron, meanwhile, stood to one side, chatting with Nico.

Both men were tall, well over six feet, but there the similarity ended. Baron was slender, and very handsome in a subdued, refined sort of way. With his wide, intelligent forehead, mild blue-gray eyes, and slow, sweet smile, he looked exactly like what he was: a fortyish, rather shy lawyer of indisputable moral integrity.

Nico, on the other hand, stood larger than life; a man who took it in his bare hands and bent it to suit his ambitions. Black-haired, dark-eyed, strongly built and tanned, he exuded raw animal magnetism at its most alluring. He had the face of a Roman centurion, all high, angular cheekbones and hard, determined jaw—and the driving will of a gladiator bound to succeed, or die trying.

By comparison, Baron was but a pale imitation of his predecessor. Not as searingly sensual. Not as wickedly humorous. And never as irresistible. But oh, so much less dangerous to love!

She relied on his steadying influence, his calm reason. He never made her feel as if she were teetering on a ledge, thousands of feet above a raging river. With him, she felt safe.

And not so very long ago, she'd thought that would be enough. She'd believed the days of wild, unfettered passion, like the turbulent teenage years, were something she'd outgrown; that she was ready for a more serene affair of the heart.

"Well, Chloe?" her mother persisted. "Just how much does Nico have to do with the way you're feeling?"

She took a last look at Baron. A late afternoon breeze blowing in from the sea played tag with his thinning hair and crept under his shirt to make a sail out of it. He tucked the shirt neatly into the waist of his trousers, and passed his hand over his hair, restoring both to order.

But Nico remained impervious, untouched. If Baron was the harbor which offered shelter from life's passing storms, Nico was the lighthouse, squarely facing whatever the elements chose to fling at him; daring them to defeat him, and relishing the challenge of the battles that might entail.

"He's got everything to do with it, Mom," she said, "which is exactly what you were hoping would happen when you invited him to stay here. But I'm not falling for it—or him. Not again. He's an adventurer, an irrepressible optimist who always comes back fighting, no matter how slender the odds of his winning. And that's not how I want to live my life anymore."

"Then everything's running according to plan?" The Prescott mother paused between sips of wine, and surveyed the company seated around the large patio table. The remains of the salmon Nico had cooked lay on a platter on a serving trolley, along with what was left of a tossed salad and a bowl of small *patate,* which he'd steamed and smothered in butter and oregano. "The wedding's taking place as scheduled?"

"Why wouldn't it be?" the groom inquired, reaching for Chloe's hand—a move which had Nico gnashing his teeth in envy.

"Oh, there's always the possibility of a slip-up

somewhere between saying 'yes' to a proposal, and 'I do' to a marriage, Baron.''

"Not for us," Baron informed his mother. "Next week at this time, Chloe and I will be in the Bahamas at the Atlantis Resort, dining on fresh Caribbean lobster, after a day of snorkeling with schools of tropical fish in the Paradise Lagoon."

"So that's where you're going." She sniffed delicately. "Since it's to be a summer wedding, I'd hoped you might choose to spend your honeymoon at the lake. You know how lovely it is there, at this time of year, how warm the water is, and how much you always enjoy swimming in it. What does the Paradise Lagoon have that's so very different from that?"

"Spend our honeymoon at the lake with you and Dad? You're not serious!"

"Well, not *with* us exactly. There are, after all, two cottages on the property, so you'd be quite alone, most of the time."

"Newlyweds usually like to be alone *all* the time, Myrna," the meekly mannered husband pointed out.

She set down her knife and fork, and regarded him sourly. "I might agree, if this were their first trip down the aisle, but spending a small fortune on a splashy honeymoon for a second marriage strikes me as being almost as tasteless as the bride wearing white."

"It just so happens that Chloe's dress *is* white," Charlotte said. "And I'm sure she'll look perfectly lovely."

"Actually, it's closer to off-white, Gran," Chloe murmured.

"As it should be," *la madre* ruled. "Under the circumstances."

Up to that point, he'd been content to sit back and observe. At this last remark, though, Nico decided Chloe's future mother-in-law had aired enough opinions on matters that were none of her business, and appointed himself to put an end to them. "I introduced Chloe to Venice on our honeymoon, but we didn't spend any time swimming in the canals, did we, *cara?*"

"Hardly," she replied, sending him a killing glare. "They were filthy."

"What else did you expect?" Myrna Prescott served up another disparaging sniff. "Venice always did carry its own distinctive…odor. The place has become such a cliché with tourists that they've completely ruined it."

"I don't consider myself a tourist, *Signora,*" he said evenly. "I have lived all my life in Verona, *La Città degli Romeo e Giulietta.* You might not be aware that it forms part of the Venetian arc. Although there exists friendly rivalry between the two cities, they are close neighbors and I have spent many satisfying hours exploring the treasures of Venice."

"And is that where you learned to cook salmon like this?" She very pointedly pushed aside the food she'd barely touched.

"*That* I learned from my mother. Veronese traditional cuisine relies heavily on seafood."

"Far too much garlic for me, I'm afraid. I find it quite overpowering."

"Perhaps you'll find dessert more to your taste," Chloe said, rushing to keep the peace. "We're having *tiramisu.*"

"More Italian cuisine? Good gracious, my dear, if

you're so fond of the country, I can't imagine why you want to marry a North American and settle down here. You'd be much happier over there.'' She mopped her mouth with her napkin. ''I'll pass on the dessert, thank you. All other considerations apart, I'm watching my weight.''

As you should! Nico told her silently. *Dio,* but the woman was a viper! And her son, was he as much under her thumb as the husband, who merely sat there looking *imbarazzato,* instead of being man enough to speak up and silence her?

Jacqueline, catching his eye and giving a barely perceptible shake of her head before quickly looking away again, spoke up then. ''In my opinion, both countries have a great deal to offer.''

''And Jacqueline should know,'' the well-meaning but bird-brained godmother, Phyllis, piped up. ''She stayed for weeks when Chloe had her little boy.''

''You have a son?'' Scandalized, the virago turned on Chloe, who sat frozen in pale-faced misery.

''Er...Mother...'' Baron began. ''This isn't something—''

But she silenced him with a peremptory flap of her hand. ''You're surely aware, Chloe, that Baron has absolutely no interest in bringing up a child of his own, let alone someone else's?''

A pity she was a woman, Nico thought, containing himself with difficulty. Had she been a man, he'd have lunged across the table, grabbed her by the throat, and shaken her like a rat.

To his credit, Baron looked thoroughly outraged. ''Drop the subject right now, Mother,'' he ordered, a surprisingly steely edge to his voice.

''I will not! You can't expect me to stand back and

watch you enter another marriage doomed before it starts, not after—''

''Do not concern yourself, *Signora*,'' Nico interrupted harshly, cut to the quick by Chloe's whimper of distress, and the way she appealed to him for rescue, her eyes so wide and wounded that his own heart clenched in pain for her. ''Your son will not be inconvenienced by mine.''

''Oh.'' The Prescott woman blinked. ''You mean, the boy lives with you, in Italy?''

''You could say so. He is buried in the graveyard of a church close by my home in Verona.''

A moment's silence spun out before Jacqueline spoke. ''We can take our coffee inside, if you prefer. I'm finding it rather chilly out here.''

At that, at last, the husband spoke up. ''Thank you, but we won't impose on your hospitality any longer, Mrs. Matheson. I'm afraid we've already overstayed our welcome. Come along, Myrna. Let's leave these people to enjoy what's left of the evening if, in fact, that's still possible. Baron, we can take a taxi if you'd like to stay.''

''No,'' he said. ''I'll drive you. Chloe looks ready to collapse. I think she's had enough for one day.''

The gaze he cast on Chloe, full of tenderness, caused a stab of regret to spike through Nico. This Baron was a good man at heart; a likable man. And he loved Chloe. He wasn't to blame for things going wrong between them, and he deserved better than to be left standing at the altar.

But Nico knew better than anyone that it wasn't always possible to control fate. Sometimes, bad things happened to good people.

* * *

"Well?" Jacqueline regarded him anxiously when, having seen the visitors off, they escaped to the kitchen on the pretext of clearing up the remains of the meal. "What did you think of that performance?"

"That the not-so-good *Signora* Prescott has made up my mind for me," Nico said, the anger still simmering. "She does not want her son to marry your daughter, *cara,* and after tonight's episode, I will do my best to see that she gets her wish."

"I hope you succeed!" Jacqueline pressed the tips of her fingers to her forehead, as if to block out the worries besetting her. "That awful business about Luciano just about put Chloe over the edge."

"So I saw." He seized her hands and gave them an encouraging squeeze. "Don't despair, *mia suocera cara.* There is hope yet that we can avert disaster."

"Oh, I hope so." She worried her bottom lip. "But we have only five days, Nico. What if it's not long enough?"

"We can't control the passage of time. We must work with what we have."

"But Chloe's pride's on the line, and she's so torn she doesn't know which way to jump. What do we do if she digs in her heels?"

"That's no reason for us to give up. What is it you say in English—the large lady has yet to join the opera?"

She smiled for the first time in hours. *"It's not over until the fat lady sings!"*

"Then how fortunate," he said, drawing her into a hug, "that all the women in your household are so slender!"

CHAPTER FIVE

Monday, August 24

SHE awoke early, almost before the sun rose. Not that she'd slept much. Who could have, after yesterday's disastrous evening?

Quietly, so as not to disturb her mother and grand-mother, she dressed in a pair of old shorts and a top, slipped through the side door behind the garage, and followed the trail through the woods, to the little clear-ing at the edge of the bluff where she'd played as a child. The tree house of her girlhood had long since disappeared, but the stone bench she'd loved as a teen-ager was still there, stained in places with a fine coat-ing of moss, and covered with the remains of last year's fallen leaves.

She swept them aside and, hugging her elbows, sat down facing the water. For long minutes, she remained utterly motionless, letting the peace and tranquility soak into her bones, in the hope that it might clear her head. Her mind was cluttered with such chaos, her emotional resources so exhausted, that she couldn't think straight.

A squirrel, traversing a low-hanging branch, squat-ted on its haunches and regarded her from bright, in-quisitive eyes. A nose-twitching rabbit popped out of the underbrush to snack on the sweet grass edging the path. To the southwest, the San Juans floated on a bank of morning mist; islands lifted straight from the pages of a fairy tale and set down on the shimmering blue sea. And all of it coming together to create the perfect setting for a happy-ever-after ending.

Was such a thing still possible for her and Baron? she wondered. Could she emerge from the maze of memories and confusion in which she was lost, and find her way back to him?

Suddenly, the squirrel chattered indignantly and scooted up the tree trunk, alerting her to the fact that someone else had approached. The rabbit froze momentarily, then hopped away to safety. A second later, Nico dropped down on the bench next to her.

Chloe wasn't really surprised to see him. Somehow, no matter how far apart they might be in miles or mood, they'd never quite severed that special intuitive connection of two people who'd once known one another so intimately that they anticipated each other's every thought. That he was there beside her now was strangely comforting; the one constant in a world gone suddenly haywire.

He didn't speak and nor, for a while, did she. They simply sat side by side, and stared across the curve of Semiahmoo Bay to Mount Baker's snowy peak, rising majestically south of the border, in Washington. Finally, without looking at him, she said, "How did you know where to find me?"

"I was walking in the garden, and saw you leave the house. I would have followed you immediately, but you seemed very pensive, and I sensed you needed some time alone."

"I did."

"Has it helped?"

She lifted one shoulder. "No."

"You're brooding about dinner, yesterday?" He made a noise deep in his throat; a growl of disgust. "The *infernale* mother of the groom, she needs to keep her mouth shut."

"It's not about her, Nico. She lives over three thousand miles away. We'll seldom see each other."

"No, it is not about her," he said, his gaze still focused on the view. "It is about you, *sì?*"

"Yes." A sigh shook her. "I have to learn to let go, to wipe out the past and concentrate on the future. I know that, up here." She tapped her forehead, then let her hand slide to her breast. "But I can't accept it *here.*"

"It is not easy to erase a portion of one's life."

"Yet you've managed it."

"You think so, *la mia bella?*" She felt, rather than saw his glance shift to encompass her. "You are mistaken. I have merely come to terms with those things I cannot change."

"How did you do that?"

"By remembering the good times," he said. "I was surprised at how many there were."

She turned to look at him then, as if, by doing so, she could draw on his strength. It was a mistake. His gaze locked with hers and wouldn't let go. It lured her very soul and, against her will, she found herself inclining toward him until his breath feathered over her face.

"And by refusing to concede defeat until the war is won," he whispered, just a nanosecond before his mouth ghosted over hers in gentle persuasion.

She knew it was madness to let her lips cling; to

close her eyes and submit without protest. Knew she should have turned aside at the last moment, and denied herself the illicit comfort of his kiss. It wasn't as if he held her and refused to let her go. He didn't touch her at all, except with his mouth. And then only barely.

But that was enough. Enough to remind her of how it used to be, before. Before it all went wrong.

When at last he pulled away, the terrible emptiness he left behind undid her. The floodgates opened, letting loose all the pent-up misery she'd suppressed for so long, and she burst into tears.

"Why are you crying?" he asked her gently.

"You know why," she said, around the sobs turning her voice harsh and ugly.

"You're thinking of Luciano?"

He remained so calm in the face of her distress, so completely in command of himself, that she flung the question back at him in anger. "Aren't you?"

"Always," he said. "But not in the way that you are. For me, the memories of our son, they shine, Chloe. I see him in the cool fresh air of morning, in the bursting open of flowers in the spring, the ripening of the grapes on the vine in early autumn. Everywhere I look, everything that touches me with its innocence and purity, reminds me of the great gift with which we were blessed. And I cannot believe such a gift doesn't still live, somewhere, somehow, and that one day I'll find him again."

"I wish I had your faith," she said bitterly, lifting the front of his T-shirt to wipe the tears from her face.

"I wish you had, too. I wish that you could heal." His voice hardened. "Perhaps then you wouldn't be racing headlong into a marriage for which you have no heart, with a man who cannot make you happy.''

She pulled away and glared at him. ''What gives you the right to make such an assumption?'' she cried, the sting of his rebuke more than she could bear just then. ''You don't even know Baron.''

''But I know you—well enough to recognize how little you're able to bring to this union. You have no raging hunger, no insatiable desire. None of the drive that makes you prepared to do whatever is necessary to hold on to him at all costs. You are in limbo, *la mia inamorata.*''

He was wrong. She was in hell, and had been ever since he'd walked back into her life! ''That's your male pride talking. You just can't stand the idea that I've found someone new.''

''Not so! What I can't stand is your self-deception. You used to be so honest, Chloe. When did you decide settling for second best was preferable to facing up to the truth?''

''I've never lied to Baron, or he to me. We've approached our marriage like mature adults, and are in complete agreement as to what we expect from each other.''

''And what is that, exactly?''

''For a start, neither of us wants children.''

''What if they happen anyway?''

''They won't. Baron took steps to make sure of that.''

''Ah,'' he said, that infuriating smile playing over his mouth again. ''He agreed to a little surgical snip-snip, did he?''

''You don't have to be so vulgar,'' she snapped.

"And you can wipe that smirk off your face, as well. Just because you're bursting at the seams with agile little swimmers doesn't mean a thing to me."

"It did once, *cara mia.* As I remember, you were rather thrilled about it."

"I've changed. The measure of a man has nothing to do with his sperm count."

"Did Baron undergo the procedure to please you?"

"No. He made the decision before we met. He's *never* wanted children."

"He might not want them," Nico declared, his tone taking on a brutal edge, "but if he marries you, he'll end up being a father anyway, because that's all you really want from him, isn't it, Chloe? Someone to lean on, someone to take care of you and shield you. Does he know there'll never be any grand passion between you, or are you doing such a good job of faking it that he hasn't yet figured out you're just going through the motions?"

"Our sex life will be just fine, thank you!"

"*Will* be?" He reared back and stared at her, his eyes dancing with evil amusement. "You mean to say, you don't already *know?*"

She sniffed scornfully, as if he'd asked the most absurd question yet to be uttered by modern man. At least, that's what she aimed to do. But the blush scorching her face put paid to her effort in a hurry.

Of course, he saw right through her pathetic attempt to bamboozle him. "You haven't made love with him, have you?" he said, feigning astonishment. "He has to settle for a chaste kiss. Or do you let him put his tongue in your mouth and touch your breasts, once in a while, just to keep him hooked?"

"It's none of your business," she replied, investing her answer with a healthy dose of haughty disdain, "and I can't believe we're having this conversation."

Unimpressed, he said, "I can't believe he's prepared to go through with this charade of a marriage. Wake up, Chloe! I might not know Baron well, but I know what a man expects of his woman. How long do you think he'll put up with a wife who's merely going through the motions, who brings no real commitment to the relationship?"

"My goodness," she scoffed. "I had no idea you were such an expert on what makes a marriage work!"

"I learned firsthand that, as long as there is love, the rest at least stands a fighting chance of falling into place." He caught her hands, turned them over, and before she could guess his intent, bent his head and pressed his mouth first to one palm, then to the other. "I learned, too, that love doesn't die just because you want it to. If it's the real thing, it endures regardless."

Shockingly, a streak of pure sexual pleasure sizzled the length of her, and settled with stunning impact between her legs. "Stop that!" she whimpered, making a feeble effort to tug herself free.

He wouldn't release her. Instead, he slid his mouth to her inner wrist, to where her pulse ran so hard and fast that it was a wonder it didn't leap out of her skin. "We had all the love in the world, Chloe," he murmured, looking up at her from beneath the dense sweep of his lashes. "It was what made the magic between us."

"But it didn't last, Nico," she said sadly. "Our son's death killed whatever we once felt for one another."

"Did it? Then why do I find myself aching to hold you again? To kiss away the shadows lurking in your lovely eyes? To feel you, warm and alive and eager, beneath me?"

Another surge of sensation bolted through her, leaving her underwear damp with yet another flush of melting heat. "You have no right to be saying such things to me now."

"Why not?" Lifting his head, he exerted just the slightest pressure on her wrists. Pulled her just close enough for his chest to brush tantalizingly against her nipples. "What I'm saying doesn't strike a chord with you?"

She sighed, capitulation sweeping over her so fiercely that she couldn't find the wherewithal to lie. "More than you know!"

"Then stop fighting it." His voice flowed around her, casting a low, hypnotic net. "Let yourself feel again, *tesoro*. Set yourself free."

Suppressing an inner shudder, she said, "I can't, Nico. I'm afraid."

"Don't be afraid. Trust yourself. Trust me."

Trust me, Baron had said. *Know that I will never hurt you.*

"Chloe…*preziosa…!*" Nico's arms went around her. His lips roamed over hers, drawing her ever closer to the edge of destruction.

"I can't do this," she sobbed, wanting to so badly that she ached with the pain of it. "It's not right!"

"It feels very right to me."

She slapped out wildly, at his chest, his shoulders, his upper arms. Anger was so much easier to deal with than fear. "Because you're selfish and don't care about anyone but yourself!"

He let go of her so suddenly that she almost tipped backward off the bench. "You are the selfish one, *cara mia*," he declared flatly. "You would shackle a man to you for no other purpose than to use him as a shield between you and anything you perceive to be hurtful. You would condemn him to a living death, just as you've condemned yourself."

"If that's what you think of me, then you should be grateful I had the good sense to put a stop to your seduction before it went any farther, because God forbid I should end up choosing *you* over Baron! But then, that's not exactly what you want to have happen, is it? Your only aim is to make me doubt myself, and spoil what I have with him."

"Why would I bother, when you're doing such a good job of that all on your own? Why *is* that, do you suppose? Because you think you don't deserve to be happy again? Is this your way of punishing yourself for Luciano's death?"

"I'm not the one who insisted on leaving him with a sitter, that night. If anyone needs punishing, it's you!"

"But of course it is," he said, his words dripping with sarcasm, and smacked his forehead with the flat of his hand. "Nico, *stupido,* how is it that you weren't blessed with divine foresight enough to realize the tragedy about to befall you? How come you're but a man, instead of God?"

"If you hadn't been so hell-bent on going out, if you'd let me stay home with him, the way I wanted to—"

"You could have done nothing. Do you hear me, Chloe? *Nothing!*" He started out softly, and ended roaring like thunder, so filled with fury and frustration that she almost cowered.

"You don't know that for sure!" she retorted shrilly. "If I'd been there, I might have realized the moment he stopped breathing, and been able to help him. But no, you had to have things your way. You had to show off by taking me to a restaurant we couldn't afford, and spending money we didn't have, and for what? Who did you think you were impressing, while our son lay dying?"

"You," he bellowed, his eyes shooting sparks, his jaw thrust forward belligerently. "*You!* But you were too wrapped up in our baby to notice. Sometimes, I think it was a blessing that he was taken from us because, had he lived, you would have smothered him with your coddling and turned him into a *mammono*— a mother's boy tied to her side by her apron strings!"

"At least he'd have known he had one parent who cared about him!"

They were hurling words at each other; using them as missiles to wound and destroy. And as the realization struck home, they sank into an appalled silence punctuated only by their ragged breathing. By mutual consent, they drew apart and stared out to sea again, because they couldn't look one another in the eye.

Seconds ticked by; became a minute, then two. Chloe knew she should leave, that she was courting disaster by exposing herself to the gravitational pull existing between them despite everything. Yet she remained motionless, too drained to move.

At length, he said quietly, "Do you remember the

last time we sat side by side on a hard stone bench in August?''

''In Verona, in the Roman amphitheater. You took me to the opera there. We forgot to bring cushions.''

''But we didn't notice. We were too wrapped up in the music and each other.''

''I'd found out that morning that I was pregnant.''

''And you told me just as Act 3 started. I missed the rest of the performance after that. You were all I could see or think about.''

''Not exactly,'' she said. ''You stood up and announced to the entire arena that we were expecting a *bambino*. You made such a fuss that people around us started complaining and told you to sit down and be quiet, or else take me home. But you said I deserved better than to spend the night in such a poor, cramped apartment.''

''So I did,'' he said, something of a smile in his voice. ''Instead, we drove into the country, to a place by the river that I'd known as a boy.''

''On our neighbor's Vespa which you 'borrowed' without asking.''

''*Sì*, and it was wonderful! You sat behind me, with your arms wrapped around my waist, and your body pressed close to mine.''

''And you sang at the top of your voice, the whole way. It's a wonder we weren't arrested for disturbing the peace.''

''I was serenading my pregnant wife. The *polizia* would have understood.'' His tone grew husky with nostalgia. ''What a magical night we had, there on the banks of the Adige. The grass and trees, the shadows deep enough to hide a couple hungry to possess one another…do you remember, Chloe?''

Remember? She could almost smell the sweet green scent of summer, the musky scent of love! If she closed her eyes, she'd see the pale glimmer of moonlight on naked limbs, hear again his impassioned murmurs and her own sighing responses. ''Vaguely. As I recall, we slept there until sunrise.''

''We made love, *cara mia,* all night long. We celebrated your pregnancy in the same way that we promoted it. With passion and tenderness. We lay naked in each other's arms beneath the stars. You cannot have forgotten that.''

Oh no, she hadn't forgotten!

''I laid my head against your belly and whispered to our child.''

He'd done a lot more than that! He'd sunk his head lower, eased her legs apart, and with an unerring instinct for knowing exactly how to arouse her, settled his mouth *there.*

''For you, little one, from your papa,'' he'd murmured, and blown gently against her flesh, to send his kiss fluttering inside her.

Already aroused to fever pitch, she had shattered into orgasm. Clamped her thighs together and held him captive at her core. And he, intimately acquainted with every nuance of her sensuality, had played his tongue over her, prolonging the ecstasy.

After, when he'd found release also, they remained locked together and watched the sunrise. ''This child will never know want, Chloe,'' he'd promised. ''I will provide handsomely for him and for you. Before long, we'll live in a mansion, with servants. You'll drive an expensive car, and shop in all the best places.''

"I don't need servants or a fancy car," she'd told him. "All I'll ever need is you."

"You have me, for now and forever."

But in the end, it hadn't been enough. When push came to shove, they'd hadn't been able to help one another. Instead, they'd isolated themselves in their separate grief, and *forever* had translated into a lifetime without the son they'd loved so dearly.

"Now it all seems so long ago," he said, with palpable regret.

She nodded. "In some ways, yes."

So long since she'd held her baby in her arms and felt his sweet breath winnowing against her neck. So long since he'd tugged at her breast, and splayed his tiny fingers over her skin. And yet, not long enough. It would never be long enough for her to accept the unkind stroke of fate which had affected her so profoundly. Even all this time later, her nipples ached and tingled, as if preparing to release her milk. She still cried herself to sleep, sometimes. A sudden reminder of what she'd lost could still leave her eyes stinging with tears in the middle of a busy day.

It didn't take much: watching a mother chase her toddler through the fallen leaves in the park; a little boy, the same age as Luciano would have been, sitting on Santa's lap in the mall, certain that life really was full of miracles.

Stirring, Nico said, "A great deal has changed in the interim."

"Has it?"

"*Senz'altro!* For a start, you're engaged to another man."

"And what about you, Nico?" she asked, glad to shift the conversation to another topic. Luciano's death was never something she could discuss with equanimity. "Is there a new woman in your life?"

"At present?" He shook his head. "No."

"But there have been others, since me?"

"*Naturalmente.* You surely didn't expect me to live like a priest?"

"Of course not."

"Yet you disapprove?"

"I have no right either to approve or disapprove," she replied, with just the right note of indifference. "You're single, and free to associate with whomever you please."

Yet the truth of her answer stung, which she hadn't expected. Somehow, whenever she'd thought about him in the years since they'd divorced, he'd always been alone. But she had only to look at him to realize the arrogance of such an assumption. He was a man in his prime; handsome, successful, confident and sophisticated. If she'd found him irresistible when he had nothing, inevitably other women would be even more attracted to him now.

"Do you think you'll marry again?"

"Of course, when the right woman is ready to say 'I do.'" He shrugged. "I am, after all, only thirty-four. I do not see myself living without the comfort and companionship of a wife for another fifty years. It is not in my nature."

Shaken, Chloe realized that *she* did not see him with anyone but herself. That he could so calmly discuss

the idea of sharing his life with another woman...!
"What about your family?" she said, hastily turning
to another subject. "Your sisters, how are they?"

"Doing very well. Carmina and Rogero had another
baby last year, a daughter at last, bringing them up to
four children. Just as well, otherwise Rogero would
have been in trouble. Abree and Chiaro have three
girls."

"What about Belva? She was pregnant when I left
Verona."

"She had a boy, Sabatino. He's four now. And since
then, there've been two more boys, Augusto, two, and
Vincenz who just turned one."

"And Delia? She has children?"

"Three. Blanche, who'll be four in December, eigh-
teen-month Milinda, and the latest, a boy, Riccardo,
just two months old."

"How lovely!" she said, working her tongue around
the bitter taste of envy nipping at her words. So many
babies, and not one of them lost!

Not that she'd wish such tragedy on anyone, least
of all a family who'd embraced her with so much
warmth and kindness. Indeed, their sorrow had almost
matched hers when Luciano had died, and they'd come
together *en masse* to try to comfort her. But she'd
barely been able to acknowledge them, surrounded as
they were by children of their own.

"*Sì.*" Nico laughed ruefully. "And how noisy,
when they all get together!"

"You must be a very devoted uncle, that you remember how old each one is, and keep tabs on their
birthdays."

"I love them," he said simply. "They are part of my family."

"I guess your mother's kept busy when they all come over for Sunday dinner."

A shadow passed over his face. "My mother died last year."

"Oh, Nico, I'm sorry! I didn't know. I remember her with such fondness. She was always wonderful to me."

He cleared his throat. "I don't know if you'll want to hear this, but her last words to me were that she would look after Luciano for you, and that he wouldn't be alone anymore."

The damnable tears, always so ready to betray her, flooded Chloe's eyes.

Dashing them away, she choked, "How like your mother to be thinking of others at such a time."

"She loved you, *cara*. We all did."

"I loved you, too."

And could again, if I let myself!

The thought rose unbidden to her mind, shocking her. It was too late to be second-guessing her feelings, she reminded herself sternly, overwhelmed yet again by the inexorable sequence of wedding preparations marching through her mind.

Ice sculptures, beluga caviar, pagoda tents, red carpets, string quartets, dance bands; the corsages and bouquets and table arrangements and rented linens and chairs; her wedding dress, hemmed and ready to be collected from the bridal boutique, her going-away outfit, her suitcases still needing to be packed...dear heaven, was there no end to it all?

"Are you happy, Chloe?" The question, gently uttered, washed over her like a shroud.

She could not look at him. Dared not. "What do you think, Nico?" she said, staring off into the distance.

"That you are the saddest bride I ever saw. That your heart is empty, and you find yourself backed into a corner from which you see no escape."

He was wrong. Her heart was full to overflowing—with regret for what, in her horrifying fall into despair, she'd left behind. For what she'd thrown away, out of fear and hopelessness. And most of all, for the fact that she'd left it too late to rectify her mistakes.

"Supposing you're right, Nico," she said, worrying the diamond solitaire on her ring finger, "what do you suggest I do about it?"

CHAPTER SIX

Tuesday, August 25

JACQUELINE phoned him just as he was heading back to his office after a lengthy business lunch. "I know you've got enough on your mind today, and can probably do without me asking for favors, Nico—"

"But you have a problem and would like my help," he finished, recognizing an uncommonly frantic edge in her voice. "What's the trouble, Jacqueline? Don't tell me Chloe and Baron have eloped?"

"Not that, thank heaven! To the best of my knowledge, he's still at Whistler with his parents. But because I had to bring my car in for servicing this afternoon, and Chloe wanted to stop by her office before she met with the landscaper at her new house, we came in together, in theory to save us bringing two vehicles across town."

"But that wasn't the real reason?"

"No. She's so hung up on all the wedding arrangements, Nico—the expense, the *material* things—that she's lost all sense of proportion. And that, I'm afraid, is my fault. She never wanted an elaborate affair, but I went ahead and turned it into a huge production anyway. I hoped, if I had some time alone with her, I might persuade her to look past all that and consider the untold cost, to herself and Baron, if she insists on ignoring the very real doubts she has that she's making a mistake in marrying him.''

"And were you successful?"

"No. She still insists it's just stress that's making her so antsy, and that she'll be fine once all the fuss and folderol is over. But you and I both know that's not the case."

"Indeed not. She is in turmoil." And frighteningly close to breaking point, as he'd realized yesterday morning when he'd drawn her into his arms. Her body had been racked by fine tremors, not easily detected by the naked eye, perhaps, but impossible to miss upon close physical contact. She was as fragile as thistle-down in a breeze, likely to fall apart without notice. And he wasn't helping matters. "Unfortunately, Jacqueline, I don't think she'll be any more forthcoming with me."

"But that's not why I'm calling. No, the problem is, my car's still being serviced and won't be ready until closer to five-thirty—something to do with the air-conditioner not working. But Chloe's stranded at the town house and expecting me to pick her up around four. I can't call her, because she accidentally left her cell phone in my car, and the telephone isn't hooked up at the new place yet."

"So you would like me to pick her up and take her home, is that it?"

"Oh, if you could, it would really help. I've got a hairdressing appointment in ten minutes, followed by a list a mile long of other things I still need to get done, and time's slipping away at an alarming rate. But I've borrowed a courtesy car, and could run most of my errands if I didn't have to worry about meeting her on time."

"Consider it done." He fished a pen from his inside pocket. "What's the address?"

She rattled off directions, which he scribbled on the back of the restaurant bill, told him he'd saved the day, and hung up.

"But who will save the bride?" he wondered aloud, dodging the traffic as he crossed the street to the tall office building on the other side.

Making his way through the crowd in the lobby, he rode the elevator to the fifteenth floor and strode down the hall to where a heavy glass door bore the *NM-Internazionale* logo. Even after two years, seeing it still gave Nico a thrill. Success and money were things he never took for granted.

Donna Melino, his Vancouver-based shipping broker, met him in the reception area. "Nico, we've got big trouble," she greeted him, something he'd already figured out from the look on her face. Normally unflappable, she was clearly agitated.

"Come into the office," he said sharply in Italian, conscious that the receptionist and junior assistant were all ears and wide, curious eyes. "Whatever it is, there's no need to advertise it to the whole world."

"I'm sorry," she said, once the door was closed and they had complete privacy. "I didn't mean to be indiscreet, but I'm afraid I'm in a bit of panic."

"I'd never have guessed!" He filled a glass with ice water from a carafe on the credenza and handed it to her. "What happened? Another foul-up on the docks? A shipment not coming in on schedule?"

"Worse." She held the side of the glass against her

flushed cheek and closed her eyes. ''That container ship you purchased—''

''What about it?''

''The sale's fallen through. I just heard from Bob Holmes, the vendor's agent. They can't deliver, after all.''

''What the devil do you mean, *they can't deliver, after all?* They damned well *have to!* They signed a contract!''

She flinched at his subdued roar, and looked at him wearily. ''Try telling that to Mr. Holmes, Nico. He'll be here momentarily. I warned him up front that he'd be dealing with you on this one.''

He paced the floor, struggling to keep his anger under control. But the ramifications of the situation went far beyond a sale gone sour. He stood to lose money— a lot of money—and perhaps more important, a reputation he'd worked hard to earn.

The prospect brought out the street fighter in him. On the surface, he might look like an executive in his tailored Italian suit; a man of moderation and reason, who never got his hands dirty. But inside, something of the boy he'd once been still remained. He remembered how it felt to be cheated.

He'd been fifteen, the first time it happened. For months, he'd saved his earnings from delivering groceries and running errands for the neighborhood merchants, all so that he could afford a Polaroid camera. His plan had been to photograph tourists and sell them instant pictures of their time in Verona. Even then, he'd been an entrepreneur.

For two weeks, he'd tasted success beyond his wildest expectations. And then, in the space of time it took for him to hand over a print of an elderly couple standing on the *Ponte Pietra,* a youth raced past and snatched the camera. Nico had given chase and caught the thief, a boy of about seventeen, both taller and heavier than he'd been at the time, but he hadn't let that deter him.

The scuffle had been brief but furious. He'd retrieved his prized possession and left his adversary bleeding in the gutter. What he hadn't known was that the kid belonged to a gang of four whose specialty was petty crime. The other three had come after him that evening, and this time the fight was longer and more vicious. He went home with a black eye, a bloody nose, and a cracked rib. But he left the others with three missing teeth, and two split lips among them, as well as enough scrapes and bruises to keep them howling for a week.

After that, word had spread: *don't mess with Nico Moretti.* It was a lesson *Signor* Holmes was about to learn.

"Make sure, when he arrives, that we're not interrupted," he instructed Donna grimly. "In fact, why don't you and the office staff leave early for once? Go to Stanley Park and enjoy the sunshine."

"Nico, you're not a juvenile, sorting out your grievances in the back streets of Verona, and let off with a slap on the wrist if you play rough," she warned.

"You're absolutely right, Donna, *la mia amica.* I've learned a thing or two since those days. Don't worry. *Signor* Holmes will walk out of here unaided—but he'll be sweating when he does so."

*   *   *

Although heat still hung heavy in the air, the afternoon had turned overcast, with ominously dark clouds scudding in from the west and banking steeply against the Coastal Range. A summer storm, Chloe thought, surveying the small, enclosed garden behind the town house. The landscape architect had proposed elaborate plans for creating the illusion of space there, with clever plantings around the patio, and a miniature waterfall trickling down the back wall into a raised pond.

Poor man! He'd become somewhat irritated by her lack of enthusiasm for the project. She should have explained that nothing much held her interest anymore—nothing, that was, except the forbidden subject of Nico Moretti.

The first fat raindrops, forerunners of the deluge shortly to follow, left black spots the size of dimes on the pale stone of the patio. Lightning flickered over the distant mountains.

Going back into the house, Chloe rinsed out her water glass at the kitchen sink, and glanced again at her watch. Almost five-fifteen. Her mother was over an hour late, probably caught up in traffic, with commuters trying to beat the storm as they headed home, but it was unlike her not to phone.

Restlessly, Chloe wandered from room to room, squaring a cushion here, straightening a painting there, but bypassing the master suite with its connotations of married intimacy. Baron had been gone two days, and she had not missed him once. She didn't want to think of sharing a bed with him. Couldn't afford the time. There was too much to do between now and Saturday.

A quarter to six, and still no sign of her mother. What could be keeping her?

Giving the towels in the guest bathroom one last twitch, Chloe returned to the second floor sitting room where she'd left her purse. Jacqueline hated talking on the phone when she was driving; said she found it too distracting. But the storm was right overhead now, turning the evening prematurely dark, and Chloe was beginning to worry.

From the window, she could see past the courtyard complex to the road. Cars swished by, their headlights throwing a bright arc ahead of them, water spraying fountain-like from beneath their tires. The wail of sirens a block or so away competed with the intermittent crack of thunder. Like it or not, Jacqueline was about to take a call.

Chloe was still rooting around in her bag for her phone when the doorbell finally rang. "Thank God!" she muttered, and ran down to the main floor foyer to let her mother in.

Instead, she found Nico on the doorstep, his expression as dark as the weather. The rain dripping from his hair joined that already staining the shoulders of his pale gray suit. The knife-sharp pleat down the front of his pants had softened to a gentle curve. *"Merda!"* he grumbled, unceremoniously pushing his way past her. "How do you live in such a climate?"

"Nice to see you, too," she retorted, furious at the way her entire body leaped with sensual awareness at the sight of him. The tumult in her stomach alone was enough to leave her feeling faint, and never mind other, less decorous parts that fairly throbbed with delight. "And just for the record, no one asked you to stop by, so don't bother taking off your jacket."

Ignoring her, he hung it on the brass coatrack and

surveyed his shoes grimly. "Save your sweet welcome for someone else, Chloe. I'm not here to make myself at home. Jacqueline sent me."

"Why isn't she here herself? What's happened to her?"

"Nothing but a slight inconvenience, which is more than I can say for my shoes. They'll never be the same again. Remind me to wear hip waders, the next time I visit Vancouver."

"Stay away from Vancouver, and you won't have to bother," she said, barring his way when he went to climb the stairs. "And what do you mean by *a slight inconvenience?*"

"She had problems with her car, and was delayed. I had expected to be here much earlier, but I, too, had other matters requiring my attention. I'm sorry if you were alarmed."

"She should have phoned and let me know. I could have taken a taxi home."

"I wish that had been possible. I have better things to do than chauffeur such an ungrateful passenger more than fifty kilometers past the city limits. But if you'd tried using your phone, you'd have realized why it was impossible for her to do as you suggest, since you don't have it with you. Jacqueline found it in her car, after she'd dropped you off at your office. So, instead of throwing up obstacles at my every word, why don't you behave like the gracious hostess you were brought up to be, and offer me something to dry off my hair? Your mother would be scandalized if she saw how you're treating your guest and savior."

Some savior! He threatened everything Chloe held dear: peace of mind, stability, security...all the things she'd fought so long and hard to achieve and thought were so vital to her happiness, but which, since he'd barged back into her life, didn't seem so important, after all.

"I'll go get you a towel," she said, being anything *but* gracious because that was the only way she could arm herself against him. "And you wait here."

Once again though, he ignored her, as she discovered when, towel in hand, she turned to leave the powder room on the second floor, and found him blocking the doorway. "Very *elegante*," he decreed, eyeing the black toilet and washbasin, gold faucets and towel rail, and deep burgundy walls appraisingly. But the mockery in his tone suggested he found the overall effect amusing, rather than chic.

"*We* like it."

"Do you?"

She flung the towel at him. "Yes!"

"*Buono*." He cast around another wry glance. "At least someone appreciates it."

Seething, she watched as he took his sweet time mopping his hair and finger-combing it into some sort of order. The sooner they were on the road, the safer she'd be.

But he quickly dashed that hope. "*Grazie*," he said, handing back the towel, then stood there regarding her expectantly.

"Now what?" she snapped, just about at the end of her rope.

"Aren't you going to give me the grand tour of this place you claim to like so much?"

"Certainly not," she said, wishing he'd move. The powder room was never meant to accommodate two

The Harlequin Reader Service® — Here's how it works:

Accepting your 2 free books and gift places you under no obligation to buy anything. You may keep the books and gift and return the shipping statement marked "cancel." If you do not cancel, about a month later we'll send you 6 additional books and bill you just $3.80 each in the U.S., or $4.47 each in Canada, plus 25¢ shipping & handling per book and applicable taxes if any.* That's the complete price and — compared to cover prices of $4.50 each in the U.S. and $5.25 each in Canada — it's quite a bargain! You may cancel at any time, but if you choose to continue, every month we'll send you 6 more books, which you may either purchase at the discount price or return to us and cancel your subscription.

*Terms and prices subject to change without notice. Sales tax applicable in N.Y. Canadian residents will be charged applicable provincial taxes and GST. Credit or debit balances in a customer's account(s) may be offset by any other outstanding balance owed by or to the customer.

If offer card is missing write to: Harlequin Reader Service, 3010 Walden Ave., P.O. Box 1867, Buffalo NY 14240-1867

NO POSTAGE
NECESSARY
IF MAILED
IN THE
UNITED STATES

BUSINESS REPLY MAIL
FIRST-CLASS MAIL   PERMIT NO. 717-003   BUFFALO, NY

POSTAGE WILL BE PAID BY ADDRESSEE

HARLEQUIN READER SERVICE
3010 WALDEN AVE
PO BOX 1867
BUFFALO NY 14240-9952

GET FREE BOOKS and a FREE GIFT WHEN YOU PLAY THE...

Lucky 7
SLOT MACHINE GAME!

Just scratch off the silver box with a coin. Then check below to see the gifts you get!

YES!

I have scratched off the silver box. Please send me the 2 free Harlequin Presents® books and gift for which I qualify. I understand I am under no obligation to purchase any books, as explained on the back of this card.

306 HDL D7WX   **106 HDL D7XD**

FIRST NAME	LAST NAME

ADDRESS

APT.#	CITY

STATE/PROV.	ZIP/POSTAL CODE

7	7	7	**Worth TWO FREE BOOKS plus a BONUS Mystery Gift!**
🍒	🍒	🍒	**Worth TWO FREE BOOKS!**
♣	♣	♣	**Worth ONE FREE BOOK!**
🔔	🔔	🍒	**TRY AGAIN!**

www.eHarlequin.com

(H-P-06/05)

DETACH AND MAIL CARD TODAY!

people, especially not when one of them was his size. He was stealing so much air, she could hardly breathe. "You're going to drive me home. Now!"

"Not as long as this rain lasts. I had to park over two blocks away, and you'll get soaked running to the car."

"So what? I won't melt."

"But I might, especially if you keep shooting sparks at me from those beautiful blue eyes."

"Stop it, Nico," she said, her voice quivering almost as badly as her insides. "We aren't going to do this again."

"Do what, *tesoro?* All I'm suggesting is you show me your new home while we wait for the rain to pass. What did *you* have in mind?"

"Absolutely nothing," she replied, exhausted with his taunting. It was easier to give in than try to match wits with him. And agreeing to show him the rest of the unit at least meant they wouldn't both be crammed in the smallest room in the house. "If a tour's that important to you, a tour is what you'll get. Follow me."

He did, more closely than he needed to, so that the scent of him—wet hair faintly spiced with whatever shampoo he'd used that morning, a lingering trace of aftershave, and summer-fresh rain—wafted around her in tantalizing invitation. Deciding the only way to resist falling under its spell was to keep three steps ahead of it, she fairly raced him through the various rooms and levels.

"That's it," she told him, winding up in the kitchen, five minutes later. "Everything there is to see. Satisfied?"

"*I* don't have to be," he replied, trapping her in his molten gaze. "I'm not the one who has to live here. But if I were faced with such a choice, I tell you plainly that I'd rather live in a tent than find myself cooped up in this tall, sterile chimney of a home, with so many stairs, and rooms so small."

"Considering where you grew up, I'm surprised you can afford to be so critical," she shot back, miffed. "As I recall, you and your sisters lived above a shop, in only four rooms, all of them tiny. You showed me where you slept as a boy, in an alcove off the kitchen."

"Because my parents were poor and after my father died, that was the best my mother could provide for us. But the windows on one side looked out on a street alive with color, and on the other to the Adige river. And there was such love and laughter under that roof that we never missed the luxuries so important to those born with a silver spoon in their mouths. But what do you have here, Chloe, apart from a high-rent address?"

He shamed her with his answer; made her feel shallow and pretentious. Looking at the house through his eyes, she saw that "sterile" suited it very well. Everything was too pristine, too perfect, and the total effect completely devoid of soul.

"It's different for us," she explained, trying to justify the sleek Art Deco furniture, the efficient stainless-steel appliances. "Baron and I are out at work all day. We'll spend only the evenings and weekends here—and even then, not always. We didn't want a place that required a lot of upkeep. Our whole aim was to be able to lock the door and go away, without having to worry about hiring a house-sitter to water plants or feed a dog.''

"Just as well." He shot a disparaging glance at the three feet of floor between kitchen counter and breakfast nook. "Even a small dog could not be happy here."

"It's an adult-oriented unit, not intended for dogs or young families."

"Adult-oriented, hmm?" He studied her, his gaze sweeping her from head to toe. "Is that why you're choosing to leap into middle age?"

"Middle age?" she choked. "What the hell do you mean by that?"

He shrugged insolently. "Well, how else would you describe yourself, all neatly repressed in your lawyer's stark black power suit, with your hair scraped back into a breakfast bun, and your eyes so empty that you might as well be dead?"

Another brilliant flash of lightning struck, occurring almost simultaneously with a deafening crack of thunder, and a second later the lights went out, throwing the area into gloomy relief. Rain pelted the skylight at the top of the stairs.

"I don't know what's put you in such a sour mood today, Nico," she told him, raising her voice above the din, and choosing to rise above the urge to stab him with a kitchen knife. "If it's having to go out of your way to pick me up, I apologize. But if you can't find something positive to say about my new home— or me, for that matter!—I'd just as soon you didn't say anything at all."

He wiped his hand down his face and sighed. "You are right, *cara.* I am not being kind. The truth is, I had an unpleasant afternoon, but that is no reason to behave badly toward you.''

Hearing the weariness in his tone, she softened. ''Something to do with business?''

''Everything to do with business.'' He shook his head and stared out at the dismal afternoon. ''Sometimes, I think I was happier when I was poor and thought I had nothing. I seldom lost sleep over that.'' His shoulders lifted in another shrug, this one laden with self-deprecation. ''Of course, when it was too late, I learned that I had more than any other man on earth, and realized the true depth of loss—but that's another story, one with which you're already familiar.''

''What happened this afternoon?'' she said, steering him away from the personal and back into the much safer waters of the professional.

''A sale I had thought was final didn't come to pass.''

''Something big?''

''A ship, Chloe. Your once-impoverished ex-husband already owns six, and had fancied himself about to acquire a seventh.''

''*Ships?*'' No amount of self-discipline could hide her astonishment or stop the gauche reply falling out of her mouth. ''Good grief, Nico, you must be filthy rich if you can afford to buy ships!''

He almost smiled. ''I suppose I am.''

''Ships…!'' Try as she might, she couldn't shake the astonishment from her voice—or quite wrap her mind around the fact that he'd managed to parlay risky, small-time ventures into a successful world-wide enterprise.

"Don't let your imagination run wild, Chloe," he advised, accurately reading her mind. "I'm not talking about Mediterranean cruise ships with swimming pools and casinos. Mine are ocean-going container ships carrying cargo from all over the world."

"So that's the reason you have business here?"

"Certainly. As you must be aware, Vancouver is the largest foreign tonnage port on the west coast of North America. My ships arrive here regularly, carrying goods from Asia, Europe and South America."

She swallowed and tried not to gape. "You must be very proud of having accomplished so much in such a short time."

"You'd think so, yes? Yet today, I am not so proud. I am ashamed. I fancy myself a gentleman of means, but this afternoon I behaved like a thug, losing my temper and threatening a man who was nothing but the unfortunate go-between for someone every bit as unscrupulous as I can be when things don't go my way."

"Why, Nico?" She sank down on the window seat in the breakfast nook, disturbed by his admission. "During our marriage, you craved success. Pursued it with a determination bordering on obsession. Why, now that you've found it, isn't it enough? Why does it matter that you weren't able to buy another ship?"

"It matters," he informed her flatly, "because it amounts to more than a sale falling through and Nico Moretti having one less toy to play with. A domino effect is taking place. My Vancouver agent has sold container space contingent upon my having that extra vessel in operation. I am unable to honor those commitments. My company's reputation is at stake. I have to subcontract the work out to another shipping line, at substantial cost to my company.''

''And money is important to you.''

It was a statement of fact, not a question, and he recognized it as such. ''I have made it important,'' he said, joining her on the window seat. ''It has driven me to where I am today. It is why I ignored the advice the experts gave me, and staked everything I had on a fleet of ugly, seaworthy vessels with plenty of cargo space. Not the kind of thing you'd choose for a honeymoon cruise, certainly, but then, I'm dealing with freight, not romance.''

''And you prefer that?''

''It suffices,'' he said, staring down some dark, invisible tunnel of regret. ''Marriage, love, they can turn on a man and squeeze every last drop of blood from his heart. Can take the things he prizes above all else in the world and turn them to dust. But if he acquires worldly possessions, he retains control of his life. They keep his bank account healthy without robbing his soul.''

''Oh, Nico, I'm so sorry!'' she whispered brokenly, grabbing his hand in both of hers. How, when Luciano died, could she have been so caught up in her own pain that she never fully understood Nico's? Why couldn't they have turned toward one another, instead of away?

''Don't be.'' Misunderstanding, he swung his empty gaze on her. ''I shall overcome this latest setback, because it has to do *only* with money. And that is something a man can hold in his hand and bend to suit his will. And if, by chance, he loses it through some unkind turn of fate, there is always more where it came from.''

''But is it enough to make you happy?''

''Does anyone ever have enough of anything, for that?'' His hand tightened over hers, crushing her engagement ring against her finger. ''Are *you* happy with all you have? With this sleek, expensive town house, with your work?'' He glanced down as she winced and tried to withdraw her hand. ''With this big diamond ring, and the man who gave it to you?''

''What if I were to say I'm not?'' she said, bringing them back full circle to the question she'd put to him yesterday. ''What would you have me do about it?''

And just as he had yesterday, he threw the question back in her lap. ''Why ask me, Chloe, when you're the only one who knows that?''

''Because I'm afraid of the answer,'' she quavered, all her carefully constructed defenses crumbling under his scrutiny. ''Because, despite everything, I'm very much afraid that I'm still in love with—''

Something slapped wetly against the window just then and remained plastered there, cutting short her confession. ''The landscape blueprints!'' she wailed, leaping up and running to the sliding door to rescue them.

They came away from the glass in soggy strips, their neat blue lines blurred beyond any sort of recognition, and clung to her fingers when she tried to spread them over the kitchen counter. ''I was supposed to keep these for Baron to see, and now look at them!'' she cried, silly, pointless tears rolling down her face. ''Now they're ruined, just like everything else to do with this marriage!''

"Perhaps destiny is trying to tell you something," Nico said, watching her. "What is it they say, about the best laid plans going astray? Maybe this is a sign. What were you about to tell me, before you allowed yourself to be interrupted?"

"I don't remember," she lied.

"I do. It had something to do with your still being in love with something." He came closer, unpeeled the paper from her hands, and pulled her around to face him. "Or was it someone, Chloe?"

Beside herself, she said, "You know it was. And you know *who* it was."

"I want to hear you say it again, and I want you to look me in the eye when you do so."

She couldn't keep up the charade. Never mind pride or decency; right or wrong. The truth would not be silenced. *"I'm still in love with you! I'm afraid I always will be! There! Are you satisfied?"*

Her words emerged on a howl of pain, and she braced herself for whatever, and however, he might reply. With amusement? Distaste?

But he did nothing, and instead let the silence spin out until she wanted to die from the shame of her outburst. "Say something," she muttered. "Tell me I'm hysterical, a fool. Just don't leave me drowning in nothingness."

"I do not have the words, *tesoro*. All I have to offer you is this."

He took her in his arms then, as if he had every right to do so. And she went willingly, because it *felt* so right to do so. For the first time since he'd stormed back into her life, she offered no resistance. Instead, she lifted her face for his kiss.

His lips were gentle. Warm, tender, life-restoring. They blotted out time, silenced conscience. They gave her courage.

Outside, the rain continued to batter against the window. Inside, her heart beat an echoing tattoo. The blood pounded in her veins. A bone-deep, aching need to feel alive again consumed her.

Yesterday faded. Tomorrow didn't exist. Nothing mattered but this moment.

CHAPTER SEVEN

Wednesday, August 26

IF CHLOE had known ahead of time that her matron of honor had planned a bridal breakfast, she'd have locked herself in her room and refused to come out. As it was, she had no idea a celebration was in the offing until she shuffled into the morning room and found her grandmother, godmother and Monica lined up, ready to squeal, *"Surprise!"*

She didn't need any more surprises. After last night, all she wanted was to be left alone—in a room with no mirrors, so she wouldn't have to look at herself and see the shame and guilt stamped all over her face.

Numbly, she allowed Monica to steer her to the seat of honor at the round table. A huge balloon bouquet floated above her chair. "I'm not dressed for a party," she mumbled, painfully aware that she was the only Cinderella in the room. Barefoot and wearing an old denim skirt and white blouse, she needed only an apron and floor mop to complete her ensemble.

"You look absolutely perfect!" Misty-eyed, Charlotte surveyed her fondly. "Doesn't she, Phyllis?"

Chloe's godmother beamed. "Of course she does!"

But Jacqueline, coming from the kitchen to pour champagne and orange juice into her best crystal flutes, looked as if her smile had been glued into place, and her penetrating gaze left Chloe squirming in her seat. "She looks exhausted, if you ask me! What time did you get in last night, Chloe?"

Had it been ten o'clock, or half past? "I'm not sure."

"You waited out the storm, I assume?"

"Yes. By then, it was well past the dinner hour, so we stopped for a bite to eat on the way home."

"I need a drink," Nico had declared, when they'd finally ventured from the town house and made a run for his car. "And from the looks of you, you could use one, too."

Her mother's glance didn't waver. "Everything went well yesterday afternoon?"

Chloe lowered her eyes, afraid of what they might betray. "Not quite the way I expected."

"But you're pleased with the outcome?"

Pleased? Hardly! What woman about to become one man's wife could approve how she'd behaved with another? Yet despite her guilt, the memory of what she and Nico had said and done last night, left her insides fluttering with forbidden pleasure.

"This is not a good idea," he'd murmured against her mouth, when that first, comforting kiss had strayed beyond the boundaries of decency into much more compromising territory.

"I know."

"We should stop now, while we still can."

"Yes."

But he continued to kiss her, and she made sure he didn't stop. She ran her fingers over the polished cotton of his shirtfront and renewed acquaintance with

*the lovely, sculpted planes of his chest. She felt his
heart thudding in time with hers.*

*Lured past all caution, she undid the buttons and
slid her hands inside his shirt. Oh, the tactile bliss of
rediscovery! Crisp dark hair and smooth tanned skin.
Muscle and bone; sinew and strength.*

"Here, girlfriend." Monica reached over, tucked a
linen napkin on Chloe's lap, and raised her glass.
"Happy breakfast, happy wedding, happy life!"

Chloe did her best to smile and project the image
of radiant bride everyone but her mother seemed to
expect. Lifting her own glass, she stared blindly at the
beads of moisture on its delicate surface.

*He'd lifted his head. "La mia inamorata," he'd
whispered thickly, his eyes devouring her, "do you
know what you're doing? Where this will end?"*

"I don't care," she'd told him.

*"But you will care, once you've had time to reflect.
You aren't one who likes to live dangerously. You've
said so yourself, many times in the last few days."*

*She'd pressed her fingers to his lips. Shaken her
head in reproof, shushing his well-intentioned warning. The intensity of his gaze had seared her. Rendered
her weak and oh, so willing!*

*Without volition, her head had fallen back, leaving
her neck exposed and vulnerable. Eyes heavy with desire, she'd watched the rain slip-sliding down the window in long, diagonal streams.*

*Then his mouth was doing the same, but tracing a
path from the corner of her mouth to her jaw, and
from there down her throat, leaving behind a chill,
damp trail that made her skin pucker.*

He ducked his head lower…lower. Nudged aside the

collar of her blouse, worried its buttons with his teeth until, frantic with impatience, she pushed him aside and with her own two hands ripped the damned things open and unsnapped the front clasp of her bra.

His mouth danced over her naked flesh, evoking lost sensation, invoking newer, greedier desire. She whimpered a soft plea. He answered with another deft touch of his tongue. Lit a fire in her that sent warmth shooting from her toes to the distant, befuddled area of her brain that cared not a whit for what was decent or proper, but craved only him.

"What happened to your appetite, dear?" Her godmother shook a reproving finger at the minute amount of food on Chloe's plate. "You need to keep up your strength. Getting married takes a lot out of a woman."

"I'm just so…overwhelmed. I had no idea you'd planned all…*this.*" Chloe eyed the tray of fresh fruit, the Belgian waffles heaped with raspberries and snowy mounds of whipped cream, the Canadian back bacon, the hot chocolate, poured from her grandmother's prized antique china mocha pot, and drunk from matching cups so delicate they were almost transparent.

She nearly gagged. Repressing a shudder, she said, "You shouldn't have gone to so much trouble, especially not with everything else that's going on this week."

"You didn't leave us much choice," Monica pointed out. "You wouldn't let me host a bridal shower, but I'm your best friend as well as your matron of honor. I wanted to give you something special to remember."

"I've tried to forget you, Nico," she'd whispered,

holding the back of his head close, to imprison his mouth at her breast.

"Some things are meant to be remembered, tesoro. You and I, together as a couple, are among them," he said, before closing his lips over her nipple.

He swirled his tongue around its beaded tip. Nipped gently at it with his teeth, then drew it deep into his mouth. The ensuing electrical charge short-circuited the last of her control. She let out a startled squeak and arched convulsively as a spasm shook her.

Growling low in his throat, he straightened to tower over her. Fleetingly, his palms cupped her breasts, shaped her ribs, smoothed over the slight curve of her abdomen, the flare of her hips.

He caught at her skirt and gathered it up, a handful at a time, until it lay bunched around her waist. Then cushioning her bottom, he brought her up snug against him; against his erection, thrusting powerfully despite being confined by his clothing.

From behind, his hand stole between her legs. They fell slackly apart, giving him freedom to wreak whatever havoc he chose. His finger caressed the strip of smooth bare skin above her stockings, and eased under the elasticized edge of her panties. Found the slick seam of her femininity. Stroked over it lazily. Once, twice.

The second spasm shook her to the core. She staggered, dug her fingers into the firm muscle of his shoulders, and clutched at him for support. He raised the pressure a notch, trespassed more deeply between the folds of her flesh. Sank his fingers deep inside her.

And all the time, from the front, he rocked against her, the rhythm of his movements measured and delib-

erate, awakening a clawing, desperate need in her. She wanted to touch him; to hold him in both her hands and return in full measure the same exquisite torment he inflicted on her.

She wanted to prolong the moment, to make it last all night and for the rest of her life. But he was making her come, and nothing she could effect could prevent the climax from gathering strength. It rolled closer; threatened to destroy her. But she wanted him to die with her. Wanted to hear again his stifled groan of defeat. Feel the hot, urgent spurt of his seed. Taste life again in its most elemental form.

Catching him by surprise, she wrestled down the zipper at his fly, and found the opening in his shorts. Already he was seeping with the prelude to full ejaculation.

Beholding his awesome strength again, feeling the heavy, silken weight of him in her hand, tipped her over the edge. Burying him between the soft inner curve of her thighs, she rode the lavish tide of orgasm. Let it wash over her in undulating waves, each more ferocious than the one before. And realized, from the sudden hot stream scalding her skin, that she had not traveled alone to that sublime and distant place. Nico had succumbed as helplessly as she.

"More hot chocolate, dear?" Charlotte held the mocha pot poised over her cup. "Or would you prefer something cooler—juice, perhaps? You're looking a little flushed."

"Water would be nice," Chloe managed, using her napkin to fan her face. "With lots of ice."

"If you're all done eating, we can get started on the fun part." Monica rolled forward the brass tea trolley loaded, Chloe noticed belatedly, with ribbon-tied boutique gift boxes.

"Now you're really going overboard," she protested. "The breakfast was more than enough."

"The breakfast was merely the introduction. This is the main event."

This turned out to be elegant trousseau items nestled among layers of tissue paper. A silky peach peignoir trimmed with creamy marabou feathers; a very brief, very sexy nightie; sheer cream stockings to match her wedding shoes; high-cut panties paneled in embossed satin and embroidered with dainty blue forget-me-nots. And perhaps the most extravagantly ridiculous of all, a Merry Widow strapless bridal corset threaded with ribbons and overlaid with cobweb-fine lace.

"You'll need nimble fingers to help you get into this," Phyllis predicted, counting the long row of hooks and eyes down the back.

"That's where I come in," Monica said. "We'll have a dress rehearsal, just to make sure we don't run into any snags on the big day. But it'll have to wait awhile because we've got something else to take care of, first."

Unable to contain her dismay, Chloe said, "Oh, please! Not another surprise!"

"Try to act like the blushing, ecstatic bride you're supposed to be, instead of a prisoner about to be given a lethal injection," Monica admonished. "Although now that I come to think about it, you're not having too much trouble blushing this morning. If I didn't know better, I'd think you had a guilty conscience."

"I do," Chloe said, grasping at the first plausible excuse to present itself. "You've got a husband and two children who need looking after. You shouldn't be here, spoiling me.''

''Your mother and grandmother did most of the work. I just gave directions.'' Monica squeezed her arm affectionately. ''Don't look so worried, girlfriend. Nothing terrible's about to happen. We just decided we'd do the 'something old, something new' thing today, instead of waiting until Saturday, that's all. By then, you'll have a houseful of guests and likely be pressed for time.'' She produced a shiny, tiny gift bag patterned with daisies. ''So here's your 'something new' from me.''

Chloe's heart flopped around inside her chest like a wounded bird when she saw the gold locket, engraved with her new initials. They'd been *C.A.M.* all her life, including the years she'd been married to Nico. There was something disturbingly final about the curlicued *C.A.P.;* it marked a definite break with the past.

''I expect you know what the 'borrowed' is,'' Jacqueline said matter-of-factly, dropping a jeweler's box into her lap. ''Grandmother Matheson's pearl and diamond necklace and earrings. They'll look quite lovely with your wedding dress.''

''And here's a blue garter,'' Phyllis tittered, swinging the ruffled item around on one finger until it twirled like a demented merry-go-round about to take flight. ''Wear it below the knee, dear, in case Baron wants to remove it with his teeth.''

God forbid! Chloe thought miserably, awash with memories of the clever things Nico could do with *his* teeth. The thought of *any* other man taking such liberties made her flesh crawl.

''I didn't wrap mine because we've been using it,''

Charlotte said, coming to sit beside her. "I'm the 'old' part, Chloe—in more ways than one, as I'm sure you're aware!—and I'm giving you my mocha set because I know how much you've always loved it. I had planned to give it to you when you and Nico…" She stopped and pressed her lips together a moment, the way a woman might, to control the onset of tears. "Well, that's another story altogether, and I've learned it doesn't do to put things off, or the chance to give pleasure to someone you love might not come around again. So enjoy this in good health and happiness, my darling, and think of me when you use it."

Chloe opened her mouth to thank her grandmother, and burst out crying instead.

"Oh, nice going!" Monica teased. "You really know how to turn a party into a howling success!"

"I'm so sorry," she choked. "Please forgive me. It's just that everything's suddenly…too much…." *Because the person whose forgiveness she should really be seeking was Baron.*

"Pre-wedding jitters," Phyllis pronounced sagely. "I've seen it often. You'll be all right, dear, once you start down the aisle. One look at Baron, and you'll forget you ever heard the words 'nervous bride.'"

"Exactly," Jacqueline said, with dismaying good cheer, as if all the doubts she'd formerly expressed had disappeared overnight. "Dry your tears, and I'll open another bottle of champagne. I think we could all use it."

Blotting her face with her napkin, Chloe pushed herself away from the table. "Let me. It'll give me something to do besides make an idiot of myself."

But her mother had already disappeared and was in

the butler's pantry before Chloe caught up with her. "Go back to the party, Chloe," she instructed, stooping to retrieve another bottle of Bollinger from the wine cooler. "I can manage this perfectly well on my own."

But, "I'm not leaving," Chloe said flatly, "until you clear up something which has me totally confused."

"Sure, if I can." Jacqueline spared her a passing glance before concentrating on stripping the foil from the neck of the champagne bottle. "What's on your mind?"

"Why are you going along with all this celebrating when, more than anyone, you've been trying to dissuade me from marrying Baron?"

"Well, there's not much point in beating a dead horse, is there, dear?" her mother replied airily. "You insist you know what you're doing, so I'm taking you at your word. If you'll forgive the mixed metaphors, it's your bed and you're the one who'll be lying on it." She set about untwisting the wire restraint securing the champagne cork, her face the very picture of innocence. "You do *know* what you're doing, right?"

"What have I done?" she'd moaned, after it was all over and they'd made themselves presentable again.

Nico, stationed at the window with his hands jammed in his pockets, had turned and fixed her in a disturbingly blunt stare. "Do I have to spell it out for you, cara? We just made love. I know that, for you, it's been a while since the last time, but you surely can't have forgotten how it feels?"

"No, we didn't go quite that far," she'd protested, making a hopeless bid to acquit herself.

"Because I wasn't inside you when I came?" Self-loathing colored his reply. *"That's a questionable technicality at best, and I refuse to hide behind it."*

"But we didn't actually... I wasn't totally unfaithful to Baron."

But Nico wouldn't let her get away with that specious line of reasoning. *"In your mind you were,"* he said implacably. *"In your heart, too, if you were telling the truth when you said you're still in love with me. Any woman who admits that to a man other than her fiancé is guilty of infidelity, no matter how she tries to rationalize it."*

Limp with despair, she'd sagged against the kitchen counter. *"So now what do I do?"*

"That's not my decision to make, Chloe."

"Is that all you have to say?" she'd cried, desperation lending a shrill edge to her reply. *"It's not your decision to make? I didn't notice you backing off so discreetly a few minutes ago, so why the sudden reticence? Are you saying that you're washing your hands of me, now that you've had your daily fix?"*

Utter disgust transformed his face. His mouth—the same mouth which had seduced her so expertly minutes before—tightened in anger, and his eyes, recently smoldering with passion, glowed with unbridled contempt. *"If that's all I wanted, there are women who would gladly accommodate me, for a price—one considerably less than you're going to exact, I suspect."*

He'd never before spoken to her so harshly; never adopted so cold and cruel a tone. But then, much about him was changed from when they'd been married. He'd become harder, tougher, in every respect. More brutal, less compassionate.

This was how he'd achieved success in business ne-gotiations, she'd realized, standing her ground with difficulty: unwilling to compromise; uncaring that he might leave his opponents crushed. "If, by that, you're suggesting I'm going to cite you as co-respondent in what just took place between us, you can relax, Nico," she said, *drawing on what few scraps of pride she still retained. "Our dirty little secret is safe with me simply because I'm too ashamed to speak about it to anyone, even a priest!"*

"You think keeping quiet about it will absolve you?" He made a sound midway between a sneer and a jeer. *"Then I pity the poor unfortunate marrying you on Saturday! And I pity you, Chloe. I thought you were possessed of more backbone and decency than that."*

His disdain lacerated her. "It's easy to despise something you don't understand, Nico, and you've never understood me. Never understood that I don't have your strength or your bold courage."

"And you think admitting to weakness exonerates you from honesty, and justifies deceiving a man like Baron?"

She looked away, unable to meet the absolute lack of respect she saw in his eyes. "You seem willing enough to deceive him. I don't hear you offering to come clean with him about the way you behaved, the minute his back was turned."

"I'm not the one marrying him. Nor do I have a fiancée waiting for me at home. I am free to do as I please, with whoever chooses to be with me at the time. And you came to me of your own free will, cara mia."

He turned the endearment into an insult. Shame-faced, she whispered, "I know that."

"And do you also know how you're going to act like the willing wife, on your wedding night? Have you thought about how you'll feel when your husband climbs into bed beside you and exercises his conjugal rights, and you cringe from his touch because he's not the man you really want?"

"Baron would never force himself on me!"

"Perhaps not, but he'd be less than human if he didn't expect you to cooperate when he finally gets you between the sheets."

"You're a pig, Nico Moretti, do you know that? You reduce everything to the level of…of…"

"What?" he'd snarled. *"A common Italian laborer, who grew up in a four-room apartment over a bakery, and should have known better than to think he could lay his dirty hands on a rich American princess?"*

She clamped down hard on her lower lip, to the point that her teeth drew blood. But even that punishment wasn't enough to still her trembling chin. "Don't you dare label me a snob, on top of everything else! I loved you for yourself, not for what you did or didn't have. And I'm sorry I made that remark about your home. You know I didn't mean it. I'd have lived in a cave, if that's the best you could have given me, and counted myself fortunate to call myself your wife."

"Until I made the cardinal mistake of proving myself fallible and no more capable of sparing you tragedy than any other man," he raged, *"and then you couldn't wait to boot me out of your life! So much for your protestations of love, Chloe!"*

"That wasn't why I left you," she flung back.

"Don't tell me it was for another man—for Baron.

I'm not sure I can survive the irony, given this afternoon's events.''

''How dare you even suggest such a thing! I invested everything of myself in you, my marriage, my son. Everything! But losing him ripped a hole in me that never healed. It left me with nothing to fall back on. I couldn't help you or myself. I was of no use to anyone.'' The anger fueling her words dwindled into quiet despair. ''Divorcing you had nothing to do with not loving you. It had to do with my own emptiness. I had nothing left to give you, Nico.''

''You have nothing to give Baron, either,'' he said mercilessly. ''I feel sorry for him, always trying so hard to please you. He will end up 'dominato dalla moglie' just like his father.''

''Dominated?'' she exclaimed, latching onto the one word that had some meaning. ''By me?''

''Exactly by you. He will be chicken-bitten.''

For a moment, she'd stared at him, bewildered. Then, understanding dawned. ''Henpecked, you mean?'' she said, so outraged she could barely enunciate. ''You're actually accusing me of being just like Mrs. Prescott?''

He gave a careless shrug. ''They do say men marry women who remind them of their mothers. I suspect you'll prove the truth of such a legend.''

''You bastard!'' She flew at him, hell-bent on wiping the smug expression off his face.

But his reflexes were quicker, and he fended her off easily enough with one hand by planting it squarely in the middle of her chest. This time, there was nothing seductive in the way his fingers splayed between her breasts, nor anything the least bit pleasurable. Instead, the two of them remained caught in a tableau defined by disillusionment and ugly recrimination.

At length, as the fight seeped out of her, he lowered his hand and said, "Enough of this. It serves no useful purpose."

"No," she agreed, turning away from him, embarrassed. "None at all."

Only in the exhausted aftermath of their own fury did they realize that the storm outside also had subsided. The rain had stopped and the shredded clouds thinned sufficiently to allow a pale suggestion of moonlight to touch the windows.

"Dio!" Nico said softly, staring out at the dark, sodden garden. "Is this what we've come to, that we lash out at each other and utter hurtful words that can never be taken back? How do two people who once were so closely attuned, find themselves so far apart that they cannot leap the distance between them?"

"I don't know," she'd wept, the ache of all they'd lost gnawing at her and laying bare her frailty. "I just wish things had ended differently. Then we wouldn't be in this place now. You wouldn't feel such disgust for me, and I wouldn't be carrying a burden of guilt that nearly kills me."

"It wasn't all bad. We knew some good times, didn't we, before everything fell apart?"

"Yes," she said, aching for those lost, enchanted years. Remember it all, she'd chided herself. Remember the pain, as well as the pleasure, or how else will you ever go on?

But memory was selective and chose to settle on the whispered words of endearment they'd shared, the tight interlocking of bodies, the deep, intense silence of completion. Of love. Of absolute faith in the future.

She let out a painful sigh. "I wish we could turn back time, that we could find our way back to what we once had."

"But we can't. We can only go forward." He shot back his shirt cuff to look at his watch. "And speaking of time, it's almost eight and we should head back to your mother's. Shall we stop somewhere for dinner, first?"

"If you like," she said, snatching at any chance to delay the inevitable. To experience another stolen hour with him, because that was the most he was prepared to offer.

Soon enough, she'd have to face the fact that, the second she confessed she was still in love with him, her already jeopardized future had spun completely out of control. Any hope she'd entertained that she could make a life with Baron had gone up in flames.

And what had been Nico's reply to her admission of love? "I do not have the words!"

But although she'd listened, she hadn't heard. Hadn't wanted to. Because what he'd really said was that he couldn't return her sentiments. He might still have found her desirable enough that he'd lost control of himself sexually, but not enough to say he still loved her, too.

He'd stripped away the intervening years, all the healing she thought she'd accomplished since their divorce, and left her with nothing. Having convinced her that marrying Baron would be her biggest mistake yet, he considered his work done, and was willing to walk away, and leave her to live with the consequences.

"It's taking you a long time to answer," her mother said, wrapping the champagne bottle in a clean white towel. "Are you quite sure you know what you're doing?"

Chloe lifted her shoulders in a hopeless, defeated shrug, ready to spill out the entire truth in all its ugliness and beg her mother's help, when the door to the butler's pantry swung open and Baron came in.

"Charlotte told me I'd find you in here," he said, pulling her back to lean against him and nuzzling her neck. "How are you, Chloe?"

"Surprised," she said, chill with horror at what he might have overheard, had he arrived a moment later. "I wasn't expecting you until later this afternoon."

"We came back early. Last night, as a matter of fact." He dropped a kiss behind her ear. "The weather changed at Whistler, making it pointless to hang around, so we headed back to town."

"You should have let me know."

"I would have, but by the time I'd stopped by the new house to show my parents where we'd be living, then taken them to dinner, it was getting pretty late."

She went cold all over. "You stopped by the town house?"

"Yes."

Totally unaware of the potential fall-out from his revelation, Jacqueline hoisted the wine bottle. "And you got *here* just in time to join the party, Baron. Care for a glass of champagne?"

"Sure," he said, after a momentary hesitation. "It's not every week that a man gets married. By all means let's celebrate."

But Chloe, still reeling from his alarming disclosure,

couldn't let it drop. "What time? What time was it when you got to the town house?"

"I can't say precisely. Eight, maybe? Half past?" He shrugged unconcernedly. "Somewhere around then."

"Seems no one was aware of time passing last night," Jacqueline remarked slyly. "Strange how that happens sometimes, isn't it?"

Chloe shot her a quelling glare. Not noticing, Baron said, "What was even stranger is that when we arrived, half the lights in the place were on. How come, Chloe?"

"I forgot I hadn't turned them off," she said, guilt at what had *really* distracted her causing unpleasant pinpricks of perspiration to speckle her skin. "The storm caused a power failure."

"So they told us, when we got to the hotel." His brow furrowed in surprise. "But that happened around seven. What were you doing, still hanging around at that hour?"

Her mouth ran dry and her lungs contracted. "We— um, that is, *I*…" She coughed lightly to cover her embarrassment, and tried again. "Well, I was…"

"I drove her into town, since I was going in myself anyway," her mother said, finally coming to her rescue, "but I ran into car trouble and wasn't able to pick her up on time."

A completely truthful answer riddled with lies, Chloe thought despairingly. Where would it all end?

"Oh." Baron nodded sympathetically. "I'm sorry I wasn't here to help out."

Not nearly as sorry as I am, she told him silently. *If you'd been here, I might still be able to look you in the eye without flinching!*

CHAPTER EIGHT

Thursday, August 27

JACQUELINE came to see him early that morning, banging on the door just after seven o'clock. "Do you know what day it is, Nico?" she demanded, when he answered.

"*Sì*. I am well aware." He retraced his steps to the kitchen, leaving her to accompany him or not, as she wished.

She wished, following so close on his heels that she almost tripped him. "Then you realize we're running out of time? That if *something* doesn't happen in the next forty-eight hours, we'll have left it too late to avert a disaster?"

When he didn't reply, but simply continued preparing his morning meal, she planted herself squarely in front of him. "Listen to me! I've tried everything with Chloe—reason, sarcasm, persuasion. As a last resort, I've even changed tactics and started acting as if this marriage is the best thing to come along since the invention of the wheel. But none of it's working, and I'm fresh out of ideas, Nico. It's up to you, now."

He heaved a sigh and swung away from her accusing gaze. "I have done enough, Jacqueline," he told her, pouring boiling water over the coffee he'd measured into the press-pot and lowering the plunger. "In all conscience, I cannot continue to make Chloe's life

124

a living hell. I have endeavored to open her eyes to the truth of what she is doing. I believe she knows that marrying Baron Prescott is no longer feasible, and that canceling the wedding is her only option. But I cannot make the choice for her.''

''You could, if you offered her an alternative.''

''Then let me rephrase my reply. I *will not* make the choice for her. I will not be the reason she does not go through with this wedding. That is a decision she must arrive at on her own.''

''But she is *miserable!* Anyone who knows her can see that.''

''She is not miserable enough. If she were, she'd do something about it.''

''What if she doesn't have the strength?''

He poured the coffee. ''Then she must live with the consequences.''

''Perhaps you can abide by that, but I'm her mother, and I can't,'' Jacqueline said, accepting the mug he passed to her. ''She's my only child, Nico, and she's suffered enough in her twenty-eight years. I can't stand by and watch her stumble into more unhappiness because she thinks it's all she really deserves.''

Seeing the distress on her face, he touched her arm in sympathy. ''Yes, you are her mother, Jacqueline, but you are also wise enough to know that you cannot always protect your child from hurt. Chloe is a grown woman. An intelligent, educated woman. She understands better than most what heartache a marriage gone wrong can cause, and not just from her own experience. She deals with such cases every day in her work. If, despite knowing this, she persists in going forward with her plans, there isn't a thing you or I can do about it. We have interfered enough. More, some would say, than we had any right to do in the first place.''

A sheen of tears filmed her eyes. ''I really thought all that time the two of you spent alone on Tuesday evening would do the trick. When nine o'clock came, and you still hadn't brought her home, I hoped it was because you were keeping her out all night. That would have been enough, Nico. She'd have canceled the wedding by now, if the two of you had made love. But of course, you'd never have let things go that far without declaring yourself.''

He could not look at her, this woman who'd welcomed him into her home and her heart, and who continued to treat him like a beloved son. *Your faith is misplaced,* he should have told her. *I do not deserve your trust or your affection.*

In truth, he could barely look himself in the eye. He'd snatched at the excuse to be with Chloe, to make one last bid for *them.* He'd done it because he couldn't let her go, because he loved her still—or so he'd told himself. But what kind of love brought a woman nothing but pain and heartache? By what right did he march back into her world and turn it on its ear?

Was it really for love, or because he wanted to punish her? Because she'd been *his* trophy, and he couldn't stand the idea of her belonging to another man? Was that why he'd refused to say the words he knew she'd longed to hear, the *I love you* which would have set her free to be with him again?

Or had it more to do with his being afraid? He didn't like to think of himself as a coward, but was there not the very real fear, buried deep inside him, that the only reason she was turning to him was to have him bail her out of her current predicament?

His doing so offered no guarantee that she'd still want him afterward. Sure, she'd said she loved him, but so what? She'd loved him before, but it hadn't stopped her from leaving him.

Jacqueline sipped her coffee, her face the very picture of distress. "I honestly don't know how I'm going to get through the wedding, Nico," she confessed. "Thank goodness a marriage commissioner's conducting the ceremony and there won't be any of that 'does anyone know just cause why this couple should not be joined in holy matrimony' stuff, because I really don't think I could keep my mouth shut."

"There's still a chance she'll come to her senses before then," he said, wishing he believed the tripe he was handing out. But he hadn't walked the floor all night because he needed the exercise. His mother-in-law wasn't the only one in agony. He was grappling with his own set of demons. He just managed to hide them better, was all.

"You think?" A sliver of hope lightened Jacqueline's expression.

"I know she is a woman of conscience, and too morally upright to enter into a binding contract under false pretenses. She will not go through the motions of marriage unless she is willing to embrace it fully, with her whole heart."

"I pray that you're right."

She wasn't the only one! He'd spent much of the last twenty-four hours making bargains with God. "There is still time, Jacqueline. What is it you told me, just the other day?"

"It's not over till the fat lady sings?"

"*Sì.*" He kissed her cheek. "And we do indeed have a fat lady, in the person of Baron's mother. Truly, Jacqueline, I cannot imagine such a harridan bursting into song. There is hope yet that all is not lost."

"I suppose," she said, returning his hug. "But I'd feel a lot better if you hadn't retired from the field."

"Let me put it this way," he said. "If Chloe decides I'm the one she wants, she knows where to find me. My door is always open, *cara.* But I cannot force her to cross its threshold."

An influx of out-of-town relatives, beginning late Wednesday morning and continuing well into the afternoon of the next day, turned the house into one long party. Chloe, caught like a piece of driftwood drawn ever closer to the eye of a vicious whirlpool, was helpless to fight the unrelenting current.

She was the bride, the center of all attention; the *reason* for all the fuss. But gripped by an emotional paralysis, she relinquished her role as guest of honor and became merely an observer, one whose fixed smile never wavered, and whose spirit was so devoid of life that she might as well have been a portrait hanging on the wall.

When everyone went upstairs to dress before dinner on the Thursday, she hadn't resolved a single one of the dilemmas facing her. Baron still believed they were getting married two days later. Mrs. Prescott, caught between sour, albeit justified disapproval of the bride, and the overweening need to show everyone she was *au courant* with her duties as mother of the groom, was still of the opinion that she was hosting the rehearsal dinner the next night.

And Jacqueline continued to behave as if she'd never once questioned the wisdom of Chloe's decision to marry Baron, and greeted every new arrival on her doorstep with a smile that stretched from one ear to the other.

Only Charlotte seemed aware that all was not well with her granddaughter, but she was too discreet to say so openly. Of course, she might have been more forthcoming if Nico had been around to encourage her, but there'd been no sign of him since Tuesday night. Once he'd succeeded in destroying any hope Chloe had of making a go of things with Baron, he'd made himself scarce, although the lights shining in the lodge at night showed he was still in residence there.

"We'll be so many for dinner tonight that I've reserved a private dining room at the Inn," Jacqueline announced to the house guests gathered on the patio for the cocktail hour. "It's only a ten-minute walk away."

"And will the groom and his family be joining us?" a second cousin, twice removed, inquired.

"Of course." Her mother shot Chloe another in her seemingly endless supply of fond and brilliant smiles. "Baron and Chloe can hardly bear to be apart. The wedding day can't get here soon enough, can it, darling?"

Chloe feared her answering smile more closely resembled the rictus of a woman suffering death throes.

The Trillium Inn, renowned for its fine dining room as well as its old-world hospitality, sat among several acres of beautifully landscaped gardens. The Dogwood Room enjoyed a particularly spectacular view of the large man-made lake where black swans floated majestically among the lily pads. Even the hard-to-please mother of the groom was impressed.

"I can't imagine why you wouldn't have held the wedding here," she fluted, over her duck à l'orange. "It's quite charming, and much more suited to a large affair such as you have planned."

"My bride wanted to be married at home," Baron said, inching his chair closer to Chloe's.

"And how about your wishes, Baron? Don't they count for something?"

"Whatever Chloe wants is fine with me, Mother," he said easily. "All I really care about is that we're getting married."

Oh, Baron! Chloe mourned inwardly, her stomach tied in such knots that she was afraid she might throw up. *You deserve so much better than what you think you're getting.*

Her face must have given away something of her inner distress, because he bathed her in a glance filled with loving concern. "Sweetheart, is something wrong?"

He was handing her the perfect opportunity to come clean, but his timing was completely off. "I need to be alone with you for a while," she hedged, excruciatingly aware that his mother sat close enough to hear every word. "We haven't had a moment to ourselves in what seems like days and there are…things that we need to talk about."

"Next week," he promised, stroking his hand up her back and massaging the nape of her neck. "We'll have all the time in the world, then. It'll be just us, the moonlight and the tropical breezes.''

"No," she said urgently. "I can't wait that long, Baron."

Mrs. Prescott didn't quite snort with contempt; she was above such things. Instead, she wagged a reproving finger and proclaimed, "If that's not typical of young people nowadays! You don't know the meaning of self-denial. You want instant gratification—preferably yesterday."

It was all Chloe could do not to bite that fat, ring-laden finger clean through to the bone. "Don't presume to tell me what it is I want, Mrs. Prescott," she said, more beside herself by the second. "You haven't known me long enough to have the first idea."

Although the general level of talk and laughter at the table was loud enough that most people weren't aware that the bride and her prospective mother-in-law had taken off the gloves and were ready to go ten rounds, the sudden lull in the conversation of those sitting closest made it glaringly apparent that Baron wasn't the only one taken aback.

Charlotte stared fixedly at her plate, Phyllis sputtered into her wineglass, and even Jacqueline's mouth fell open in shock. The only person unaffected by Chloe's outburst was Mr. Prescott, who continued to chew his way stolidly through the steak he'd ordered.

"Perhaps not," his wife said, dropping her reply, syllable by crystal-clear syllable, into the small well of silence surrounding her. "But I do know my son, and he is not given to the rather bizarre impulses which seem to be part and parcel of *your* makeup, Chloe. I refer not just to the here and now, but more specifically to the afternoon we found you cavorting in the pool with your ex-husband. I can't help but think that, although Baron might presently consider such odd behavior charming, he will find it tiresome, once the novelty wears off.''

"That's enough!'' Baron, normally so mildly spoken, issued the order with the crisp authority of a sergeant major. ''You will apologize to Chloe for that remark, Mother.''

''No.'' More embarrassed than she'd ever been in her life before, Chloe laid a hand on his arm and turned to his mother. ''I'm the one who should apologize, and I do, Mrs. Prescott, most sincerely.'' Her mouth trembled and she made a monumental effort to control it, before continuing, ''I'm afraid I'm not myself tonight. I haven't *been* myself for quite some time. Please forgive me.''

Mrs. Prescott hesitated fractionally, then inclined her head. ''Certainly. I'm sorry, too, if I spoke out of turn. I'm afraid weddings are emotionally taxing, not just for the bride, but for the mothers whose children are about to take such a life-altering step.''

''It doesn't have to be like that, Myrna,'' Baron's father stopped chewing long enough to remark. ''It's all a matter of how you look at it.''

Ignoring him, she turned again to Chloe, an unexpectedly compassionate gleam in her cool gray eyes. ''Men just don't understand, do they?'' she said quietly, as if she and Chloe were the only two people in the room. ''They just take everything at face value, and never bother to scratch below the surface to find out what's really going on. But we know better, my dear. We might fool ourselves for a little while, but eventually we have to confront the truth, regardless of how painful it might be.''

Chloe met her gaze head-on. "Yes, we do."

"Then I apologize again for my previous comment." She held Chloe's gaze a moment longer, then gave a tiny, conspiratorial nod. "If you and Baron have matters to discuss once dinner is over, his father and I will take a taxi back to our hotel."

"Thank you." Chloe turned pleading eyes on Baron. "May we please do that?"

"No," he said flatly, even though his calm smile never faltered.

Stunned by his refusal, she said, "But it's important, Baron."

"I'm sure you think so, but it's going to have to wait a few more hours."

"It can't!" she insisted. "You don't understand—"

"But I do, Chloe, much better than you seem to realize. All these weeks of wedding preparations have left you worn to a shadow. More than anything else, you need rest, my love. Whatever it is that has you looking so wretched won't seem nearly so bad after a good night's sleep."

He spoke with such kindness, looked at her so sorrowfully, as if, deep down, he already knew his hopes of a happy ending with her grew slimmer by the second, that her heart almost broke. How could she let him down at this late date and live with herself afterward? Surely, if she tried very hard, she could make *him* the one to haunt her dreams, the one she wanted with desperate, driving hunger?

His gaze roamed over her face as if he were committing every last feature to memory. "Please don't look so anxious,'' he murmured. ''I promise you, everything will be all right. One way or another, we'll sort out whatever's troubling you.''

She wanted to believe him. Had never wanted anything as much in her entire life…except for Nico. Dear God, what kind of monster did that make her?

Still in a festive mood when they returned from the Inn, the house guests weren't at all interested in making an early night of it. More wine flowed, music filled the downstairs rooms, someone started a conga line. And suddenly she was the only one not taking part.

''Come on, Chloe!'' they urged, laughing, and dragged her into the middle of the floor. ''Live it up while you can!''

They all wanted so badly for her to be happy, that it pained her to look at them. Trying to match their smiles was as impossible as staring into bright, oncoming headlights and trying not to squint.

Perhaps Baron had been right in refusing to let her talk to him tonight. Although outwardly serene, inside she was like a wild animal, trapped and running blindly in all directions, seeking escape. But no matter which way she turned, she ended up banging into the bars of the cage containing her—except that, in her case, they were bars of her own making, and until she broke them down, she had no right inflicting pain on anyone else. One way or another, she *had* to resolve her fluctuating ambivalence, and put an end to the maelstrom of emotion tearing her apart inside.

Unwilling to give rise to unwelcome speculation and injured feelings by openly shunning the party, she chose her moment when everyone was admiring the wedding gifts, muttered the excuse that she needed a breath of air, and slipped through the French doors to the garden.

Once there, she simply opened her consciousness and let the tumult of her thoughts run wild in whatever order they chose. One strand overlapped another, untangled again, and eventually came together in a certain logical sequence that hinged entirely on one thing: love.

She'd learned years ago that it wasn't simple or easy. It didn't die on command. Despite her best efforts not to do so, she still loved Nico. She'd always love him. How could she not, when he was her son's father?

Yet that didn't preclude her loving Baron, too. Not quite the way she loved Nico, perhaps—nothing would ever equal that blind, youthful intensity—but sincerely nonetheless, and deeply enough that the thought of hurting him made her physically ill.

He was such a good man; such ideal husband material. They'd started out as colleagues, become good friends, and on that solid foundation of mutual respect gradually made the transition to romance.

She'd loved his integrity, his sense of fair play, his dry humor and unfailing good temper. Wearing his ring had made her proud, and if fireworks didn't explode around her when he kissed her, that was all right, too. He was, after all, a man of contained passions. It was what made him such a good lawyer.

But sex would be good between them. Not earth-shattering, the way it had been with Nico, but good just the same. Baron would be a tender and considerate lover. If there weren't any soaring highs with him such as she'd shared with Nico, she knew for certain that there'd be none of the despair-filled lows, either.

She'd thought it was all she ever wanted: to know that she'd never again have to visit that dark and dreadful place of grief; to live with the sure knowledge that she wouldn't be blindsided by a vicious stab of sorrow because she happened to look at her husband's face, and see there a living resemblance to the child she'd lost.

All those reasons remained valid. None of the fine qualities which had drawn her to Baron in the first place had lessened since Nico had come back on the scene. If anything, she esteemed him even more for the generous way he'd accepted the presence of a man few other people would have tolerated.

She tried to imagine not having him by her side, and could not. Could not begin to comprehend the gaping hole his absence would leave in her life. Yet she was tormented beyond endurance by longing for another man.

If only Nico would disappear and never come back! If only she could scour away the memory of that scene in the town house, on Tuesday, and the residual guilt that went with it!

If only she could stop loving him!

Music filtered from the open windows of the house, a number from the soundtrack of *Mamma Mia,* so haunting and unbearably beautiful that she wanted to weep.

Clapping her hands to her ears, she ran down the brick path, to the gate beyond the rose garden. A lilac hedge rose up on the other side, its blooms long since withered, but its leaves offering concealing sanctuary from anyone who might be watching at the house.

Pushing the gate open, she went through and huddled at the far edge of the lawn fronting the lodge, at the place where it sloped down to the edge of the cliff overlooking the Strait.

How long she stood there, her chest heaving, the tears rolling down her face, she couldn't have said. Gradually, though, she became aware of footsteps approaching and coming to a stop directly behind her.

She knew without looking that it was Nico because every pore in her skin responded to his nearness. Every pale and tiny hair on the nape of her neck quivered to attention. The very air crackled with silent electricity.

Do not turn around, she commanded herself.

Strong masculine hands closed over her upper arms. A voice uttered her name. Nico's hands, Nico's voice, resurrecting near-forgotten memories of the warm, sweet night breeze of Verona sweeping softly over her naked body, and moonlight throwing dusky blue shadows over her skin. And Nico, limned in the pale light like some ancient, beautiful god come to steal a mortal's soul, hovering above her, murmuring words of love that fell from his lips like music…*tesoro… angelo…la mia moglie adorata…te amo….*

She squeezed her eyes shut, so tightly they stung.

Do not acknowledge him…!

His lips settled quietly at the spot just below her ear. Slid in a smooth arpeggio down the side of her neck, and from there to the curve of her shoulder. His lashes fluttered against her skin, a charming, alluring afterthought that left a trail of goose bumps in its wake.

Do not let him in…!

Even though her flesh burned where he touched it, even though every nerve in her body jumped in shimmering anticipation of a pleasure she'd only ever found with him, she could not let him know.

Baron was the better choice, the man who offered her the constancy she craved. *He* was the one who should be seducing her softly.

But it was Nico who ran his palms down her night-chilled arms and laced his fingers in hers. Nico who whispered sweet Italian nothings in her ear.

Do not listen! Do not turn around!

But her body didn't hear. Didn't care. Instead, it took on a life of its own, swiveling in response to the persuasion of his hands, and bringing her face to face, breast to chest, hip to hip, with the one man in the whole wide world to whom she'd never been able to say "No."

"What are you doing out here, all by yourself at such a late hour?" he asked, the question whispering over her mouth like a breeze.

"I have nowhere else to go," she replied brokenly.

Without another word, he swung her off her feet, cradled her against his shoulder and covered the distance to the lodge in long, swift strides. The magnolia trees and lilac hedge blocked out the sight of the main house. The sleepy swish of the waves rolling ashore drowned out all the music except for the anthem beginning in her heart.

Reason couldn't dictate the right or wrong of it, because there was nothing reasonable about the wild anticipation thrumming through her veins. The one true voice she heard was that which told her she was where she belonged.

He didn't pretend to bother with social foreplay. No offer of a glass of sherry to warm her shivering body, of conversation to ease her afflicted mind. Instead, he kicked the front door closed behind him and marched straight up the stairs to the bedroom.

The windows stood open, letting in the sweet, heavy perfume of night-scented stocks and nicotiana. Only a smattering of stars winked between the branches of the copper beech outside, and the moon, just rising, offered next to no light at all. But a lamp on the dresser cast enough of a glow to penetrate the shadows of the room. Enough that she could see the passionate curve of his mouth as he lowered her to the floor, his heavy-lidded gaze as it traveled the length of her, the slow rise and fall of his chest.

His hands circled her waist. Inched her toward him until she stood close enough for his breath to winnow over her face. The slow torment it inflicted left her whimpering helplessly. She lifted her mouth to his, mutely begging to be kissed. But he continued to toy with her, hovering but never quite touching.

Then, after what seemed like forever, he brushed his lips across hers—one way, the other, like a bird unable to decide where it wished to settle. A fleeting taste of heaven here; a brief, burning promise there. A swift, openmouthed sweep, warm and wet across her parched lips, followed by tormenting withdrawal, and another long, silent scrutiny from eyes so dark and shadowed she hadn't a hope of reading what lay in their depths.

"I hope you know what you're doing, Chloe," he said at last, his voice coated in sugared gravel. "I hope that, this time, you're quite sure I'm the one you want and there aren't going to be any recriminations flying, afterward.''

Her breath caught on a splintered sigh. She framed his face between her hands so that he had to look at her, had to see the truth she knew he'd find written on hers. ''I'm sure.''

If permission was what he'd been waiting for, he heard it in her answer. Felt it in the urgency with which she pressed herself against him. The time was past for leisurely explorations; for *almost* touching, *almost* kissing.

With a low growl of satisfaction, he ripped down the zipper of her dress, tugged at the bodice until it fell around her waist, then walked her backward until she fell across the bed with him on top of her.

In the throes of her own wild need, she tore open the buttons on his shirt, pressed her eager mouth against the smooth curve of his shoulder, slid her hands inside the waist of his pants, and over his taut, slim buttocks.

''I want you naked,'' he muttered between fevered breaths. ''I want to feel all of you underneath me.''

And so it was. Clothing tossed aside haphazardly. A brief, breathless suspension of time while they devoured each other with their eyes, renewing acquaintance with physical features they'd once known so intimately that they'd have recognized each other by touch alone in a crowd of thousands.

How could she have forgotten the slight bump along his collar bone, broken in a game of street soccer when he was nine? The tiny raised scar just above his ribs, the legacy of a fight when he was in his teens? The imposing width of shoulder, the narrow waist, the way the crisp haze of dark hair on his chest softened to silk as it narrowed down his flat belly, then flared again to nest around his manhood?

How could she have thought for a second that *any* other man could ever raise her to painful, quivering expectation just by the sight of his powerful, vibrant arousal? Nico was strong, in mind and body; a force to be reckoned with regardless of most circumstances. Yet when it came to mastering his sexual response to her, *she* was the one in control.

Barely had the thought taken root, though, before he reminded her of the other half of the sexual equation between them. His fingertip, running in a straight line from her throat to her navel with a feather-light touch that barely grazed her skin, made her gasp aloud. A rush of heat pulsed through her body, leaving her thighs shaking and the folds of flesh between them puddled with excitement.

"You are still beautiful," he allowed, knowing she had learned her lesson, and that there were never any winners when it came to making love.

Wanting to punish him with similar pleasure, she let her finger skate from the indentation separating the muscled planes of his chest, and all the way down his torso until she found the sleek, vulnerable tip of his penis. "And you, Nico."

The breath hissing between his teeth marked the end of the preliminary skirmish. No more holding back after that. No more questions, no more *thinking*. Just him and her, skin to skin, the way it was meant to be. Mouths seeking, tongues playing, unhindered, wherever they chose to go.

The taste and texture of him, pure male, pure sex, drove her wild. His fractured gasp of pleasure when she took him in her mouth, his steely determination not to submit to her torture...oh, they made her feel victorious, invincible—until, again, he exercised his own exquisite form of mastery and brought her tumbling into submission.

Effortlessly, he flipped her onto her back so that she lay spread-eagled beneath him. He knelt astride her. Probed gently with his hard, heated flesh at the juncture of her thighs. Slid easily between their welcoming inner curves, then withdrew again, a nanosecond before penetrating farther. Flirted with her repeatedly, each time tossing her closer to heaven.

She thrashed beneath him, inarticulate sounds issuing helplessly from her throat as the encroaching waves of orgasm threatened to engulf her. She could not hold them back, and yet, by themselves, they were not enough to satisfy her. She wanted him—*all* of him—deep inside her. Wanted to welcome him with her own flesh convulsing around his.

She flung out her arm, as if by doing so, she might tame that part of her body refusing to submit to patience. She succeeded in a way she could never have anticipated.

Her fist cracked against glass. Shocked, she turned her head and saw she'd struck a brass picture frame on the bedside table, hinged down the middle and containing two photographs. The first was of her, silhouetted by sunshine and hugely pregnant; the other of Luciano, taken shortly before he died.

Never again, she'd vowed, when Nico, desperate to avoid the divorce and somehow put right a world forever gone wrong, had suggested that, in time, another baby might help ease her pain. *Never again!*

Yet here she was, so bent on finding escape from today that she hadn't given a thought to tomorrow's possible consequences. She'd ignored logic for instinct, and it had led her straight to the brink of disaster again. Good God, would she never learn?

CHAPTER NINE

Friday, August 28

HE MADE a note of the flight information he needed, and replaced the phone in its cradle. It was over. Done.

Once the anger subsided—and it had been directed at himself, more than at her—he'd known exactly what his next move had to be. Now that he'd taken it, he felt better. Less morally reprehensible, although not entirely guilt-free. But that was the price a man paid for putting his integrity on the line, and acting against his better judgment for a woman he'd once loved with an all-consuming passion.

Well, no more. She wasn't the only one who'd changed. This time, he wouldn't beg, and he wouldn't sacrifice his own needs in order to satisfy hers. If she was bound and determined to screw up her life...well, hell! It was hers to do with as she pleased, and all he could do at this point was let her get on with it.

"Sorry, Chloe," he'd said the night before, not even bothering to go downstairs and see her out. "You're the one who showed up outside my door, this time, certain you were where you wanted to be. I did my best to give you what you said you wanted, and once again, at the last minute, you backed off."

"You know why," she cried. "And it had nothing to do with my not knowing what I want."

"Perhaps not. Perhaps, this time, it's a matter of my

knowing what I *don't* want. It's over between us, Chloe. I'm finished with this whole mess.''

''Just like that? You give me an ultimatum and there's no room for negotiation?''

''None at all,'' he told her, unable to look at her tear-stained face for fear he'd cave in. ''I'm all talked out.''

She'd left without another word. He'd watched her go, knowing that, this time, she was walking away for good, and he would do nothing to try to bring her back.

It was better this way.

''So…!'' The next morning, Baron slid into the empty chair across from Chloe's in the restaurant, and shook out his napkin. ''Getting together for breakfast was a great idea. I'm glad you thought of it. Did you order for me?''

''Yes,'' she said. ''Unsweetened grapefruit juice, two poached eggs, dry toast and black coffee.''

He smiled. ''You know me so well, Chloe. We're going to do very well together.''

''Baron—''

''Are you all set for the rehearsal dinner tonight?''

''No. I'm—''

''Not that we're having a rehearsal, as such.'' Another smile, slow and sweet and heartbreaking. ''We've both done this before, after all. We know the ropes. I suppose, to be accurate, we should be calling tonight's affair the groom's dinner, and leave it at that.''

''Baron, I can't go through with it.''

''The dinner? Of course you can, Chloe. My mother's promised to behave herself.'' He made a big production of perusing the menu. "You, know, I think I might change my mind and have the eggs Benedict."

"Not the dinner, the wedding." The words fell out of her mouth as bald and clumsy and cruel as bricks smashing through crystal. "I have to call it off, Baron. I'm so sorry. And so ashamed."

He buried a sigh and put the menu to one side. "I was afraid this might happen."

Too engulfed in misery for the resignation in his answer to register fully, she spread her hands in a hopeless gesture, as if they might convey the regret no words could adequately express, and said again, stammering this time, "I truly am so very sorry! I wish I didn't have to do this to you."

"Are you quite sure that you must, Chloe?"

"Yes. It's the only honorable thing I *can* do. If I weren't such an abysmal coward, I'd have spoken sooner. But I kept hoping…" She tried to swallow the humiliation threatening to choke her. Wished she could offer a reason that would exonerate her from culpability, and knew there was none. "I kept hoping things would work out for us, and if they couldn't, then that some*one,* or some*thing* else would make it impossible for us to go through with our plans, so that I wouldn't have to be responsible. I'm not proud of myself for that, Baron."

"When did you reach your decision?"

"I knew for sure last night." She ventured a glance at him, the import of his earlier response finally hitting home. "And you don't seem too surprised."

"I might not be the most brilliant man in the world, Chloe, but I'm not completely lacking in perception. I knew the moment Nico came on the scene that it was only a matter of time before you realized you couldn't marry me.'' He shot her a look of such utter sympathy that she flinched. ''If anyone should apologize, I should, for not having let you off the hook sooner.''

''Oh, please, Baron!'' she said, struggling for composure. ''Please don't make me feel any more ashamed than I already do. This was my responsibility to shoulder, not yours. And to be fair to Nico, I can't lay all the blame on him. I was having doubts before he showed up. He just made me face up to them.''

Baron laid a consoling hand on her arm. ''Listen to me. You've had a great deal to contend with in the last month, buried as you've been in a steady stream of wedding details that left you no time to stand back and gain any sort of perspective. But I have no such excuse. I saw the chemistry between you and Nico— I'd have had to be blind not to!—and I did nothing. Instead, I stuck my head in the sand and chalked it all up to wedding nerves. So you see, I'm an even bigger coward than you, Chloe.''

''I think you're saying all this just to be kind and make me feel better.''

''No, I'm telling you the truth. This wedding took on a life of its own and steamrolled over anything that got in its path. You didn't know how to stop it, and I didn't care to try.'' He patted her arm one last time, then withdrew his hand. ''I won't pretend my pride isn't taking a bit of a beating, but I promise you I'm not about to drive my car off a cliff or overdose on antacids. You and Nico can go ahead and start over with my blessing.''

''No, we can't.'' She hung her head, hating what

she knew she must add. But Baron deserved to know the full truth. "He...doesn't want me."

"Not like this," Nico had raged, when their love-making came to a sudden and premature end because she'd undergone another last-minute attack of scruples. *"Damn you, Chloe! Come to me because you can't stay away, not because you need an excuse to leave Baron!"*

"Why does it have to be all or nothing with you?" she'd cried.

"Because that's the kind of man I am. I'm not interested in being your temporary savior, someone you need for just a little while. I worked too hard to come to terms with your walking out on me once before, and I'm not about to go down that road again."

"What if we could make a real go of things, this time?"

The scorn in his laugh had flayed her to the bone. *"With your screwed-up approach to coping? Not a chance!"*

"Why not? Because I wouldn't have sex with you tonight unless you used a condom?"

He'd laughed again, more bitterly than ever. "If this was just about tonight, I'd insist on using one. But it's about tomorrow and next month and next year. It's why you're all set to marry Baron—because he's willing to settle for half a life with half a wife. Well, not me, sweet face! I want a woman who's brave enough to face the future without having it sugar-coated in a guarantee that it'll always be safe and perfect and free from pain. A woman who stares destiny in the face and defies it to strike against her a second time."

"Are you saying you want more children?" she'd asked, her voice hushed with trepidation.

"You bet I want more children! I won't let one unkind stroke of fate reduce me to a whimpering coward. What the devil does a man work for, if not for a wife and children? What the hell else is there that amounts to a damn thing worth having?"

He'd seen the doubt on her face, and his own had contorted with disdain. *"Your trouble is you've been spoiled your whole life, Chloe. Coddled to the point that you take each and every setback as a personal affront, and I'm as much to blame for that as anybody. But, guess what? You're not the only mother to have lost a child. It happens all the time to other women. The difference is, they don't let it cripple them. They grieve, and you can bet they never forget, but eventually they get up and go on living. But you…you might as well have died with our son because you're right. You don't have a damned thing left to give to anyone else."*

She'd known he was capable of rage, had seen him grapple with it when Luciano died, but never had she expected him to direct it at her with such unbridled contempt.

"If this is how you really feel, I don't know why you bothered to open your door to me tonight."

"Because I feel sorry for you," he'd said, wiping a weary hand down his face and sounding as drained as she felt. *"Almost as sorry as I do for the man you're about to marry. Thank God it's Baron and not me!"*

"I wouldn't have you if you were the last man on earth!"

"Good, because I'm not offering! You want a pain-

less life, and I know better than to think I can give you one, because there is no life without pain. How does anyone learn to savor the good times, if they never learn to cope with the bad?''

She'd started to cry then, hopeless, helpless tears that just wouldn't stop. He might not have come right out and said so, but he despised her, and who could blame him? Good grief, she despised herself—for her weakness and timidity and dishonesty. He was right. She was afraid—of him, of herself, of living life to the fullest—and quite willing to hide behind someone else so that she never had to face up to her fears.

He'd watched her dispassionately for a while, then handed her a tissue from the box beside the bed, and said, "Go home, Chloe, and do yourself a favor. Unless you want to wind up in the divorce court a second time, take a long, hard look at what you're asking of yourself and Baron, by going ahead with this marriage."

"What do you care," she'd sobbed, "as long as you don't have to clean up the mess?"

"I don't care," he said flatly. "But only because I won't let myself."

"And if Nico did want you, would you go with him?" Baron asked now.

"No," she said, the endless tears of the previous sleepless night having at last washed away all the clutter from her mind and left it receptive to the kind of brutal soul-searching so long overdue. "I've been running away from myself for a long time now, and it has to stop. I don't much like the person I've become, Baron. I've never thought of myself as a user, but I'm afraid I've taken unconscionable advantage of you *and*

Nico. The difference is, he won't let me get away with it, whereas you always make allowances, always show yourself ready to settle for what I'm willing to give, without once asking for more.''

"You don't hear me complaining, Chloe. And in all honesty, neither of us has ever pretended ours was the love match of the century. I think we both know that's something that rarely happens in real life."

"But it *did* happen to me, that's the trouble. I know how it feels to love a man so madly that he fills my dreams and occupies my every waking thought to the exclusion of everything else.''

Baron beat his fingertips in a soft tattoo on the linen tablecloth. "Perhaps that's where we differ the most, then, because I'm not sure I'm capable of that kind of passion. I'm not sure I ever want to be," he said thoughtfully. "That's why we made such a good couple—or at least, I thought we did. But I've seen another side of you this last week, Chloe, and I realize I was wrong. The real you has been undercover all this time, and it took Nico to bring you out of hiding.''

"It's not that I don't love you, Baron, because I do," she said, hating that she sounded so trite and condescending.

"I love you, as well. You will always be very dear to me. But you know, I've been divorced for over thirteen years and I have to confess that there've been times when I've questioned my ability to give up the rather solitary life I've enjoyed for so long.''

"You say that now, because you want to make me feel better about jilting you at the last minute, but if I hadn't called off the wedding, you'd have gone through with it.''

"Yes, I would have. As I said before, you're not the only coward in the mix, Chloe. I'd have gone ahead and made the best of things, and I don't suppose it would have been too difficult. We are, after all, very good friends." He smiled again. "Perhaps that's all we were ever meant to be."

"You're one of the finest men I've ever known, and your friendship means more to me than you'll ever know." She shook her head, her relief at having at last done the right thing diluted by a terrible feeling of regret for all the hurt she'd caused. "So where do we go from here?"

"I suppose the first thing is to cancel as many arrangements as possible. Have you told anyone else what you've decided?"

"No. The least I could do was let you be the first to know."

"Then I suggest you tell your mother and grandmother next. Let them help you. I'm sure they won't—"

"There are bigger issues at stake than canceling the wedding arrangements, Baron! What about the town house, and our working together?"

"The real estate market's very hot right now. We'll have no trouble selling the house. As for working together, there's no reason we can't go on as before. It's not as if we see that much of each other in the office, anyway." He regarded her over the rim of his coffee cup, a glimmer of amusement in his eyes. "In any case, I rather think you'll be leaving the country eventually. It's a very long commute from here to Italy."

She started crying again at that, overwhelmed by a generosity she didn't begin to deserve. "If that ever happens,'' she said, dabbing at her eyes with her napkin, ''I'm going to miss you very much.''

By noon, the most urgent phone calls had been made, and word that the wedding was officially off had gone the rounds. There was a host of details still needing attention, of course, perhaps the most time-consuming being to return wedding gifts with an appropriate note of thanks and explanation. But the most onerous task in Chloe's opinion, once she'd spoken to Baron, was facing Nico again.

She didn't expect him to fall all over himself just because she'd finally had the guts to do what she should have done at least a week ago, if not before. But she hoped she could at least regain a little of his respect.

Any such notion died as she pushed open the gate at the bottom of the garden. Such an air of quiet solitude enveloped the lodge that she knew what she'd find, even before the front door swung open to confirm there was nothing behind it but empty rooms. He was gone, not just to walk on the beach, or attend another business meeting downtown, but *gone*—as in *left completely, never to return.*

The kitchen was spotless, the cushions on the sofa in the sitting room tidily in place, the clothes closet empty. Nothing remained to remind her that he'd been there, except for the sheets and towels dropped in the laundry hamper in the bathroom—and the photograph of her, which he'd removed from the double picture frame and left torn in half on the nightstand as a telling finale before he'd rung down the curtain on their relationship.

If there was to be a sequel, she'd have to be the one to enact it, and for both their sakes, it couldn't be soon. Aware of the risk invited by delay, because there surely were legions of women who'd be happy to fill the shoes she'd left empty, it was nevertheless a chance she'd have to take. Nico wanted a partner able and willing to share the load, and until she could offer him total commitment, she had no right to importune his love.

I don't care, he'd said last night, shortly before he'd booted her out of his life, *but only because I won't let myself.*

It wasn't much on which to pin her hopes for a happy ending to their love affair, but it was all she had, and she clung to it as she faced the long road of recovery ahead.

The wedding didn't happen, after all, Jacqueline wrote, at the beginning of October. *Just as we hoped, Chloe came to her senses at the last minute, and it didn't seem to come as much of a surprise to anyone, least of all Baron. They remain good friends and colleagues, and though it was all a bit frantic for a while, everything's settled down now. She moved into her own place last week, a condominium on the west side, and plans to spend Christmas in Mexico. She never mentions you, Nico, and I don't ask, but Charlotte and I both so hoped the two of you would kiss and make up. Perhaps, the next time you come over here, you'll find a way....*

It wasn't going to happen. He'd appointed Donna Melino CEO of his North American operation, leaving him free to concentrate on his other business holdings and his nonexistent private life. He'd suffered punishment enough at Chloe's hands, and only a fool would keep going back for more. It was time he shed the emotional baggage he'd carried around for so long, and made a fresh start with someone whose wounded, reproachful eyes weren't a constant reminder of all he'd lost.

While she was sunning herself on the Mexican Riviera, he'd be actively shopping for a new wife. The next time a wedding was in the offing, it would be his.

Trouble was, although women were easily come by, finding one who held his attention for more than a week or two proved next to impossible. Either they were too much like Chloe, or not like her enough. When the new year rolled in, he celebrated with his sisters and their families, and was the only man at the party who didn't have a woman in his arms at midnight.

"Your problem," his brother-in-law Hector told him, in a hung-over bout of confidence the next morning, "is that you want to turn back time. You want Chloe the way she used to be, before your little son died. But you know, *l'amico,* losing a child changes a person forever. You're not the same man she married, either."

"It doesn't take a genius to figure that out," he'd replied shortly. "You've only got to look at me to see I've changed."

"I'm not talking about the fact that you appear more successful on the surface. It's what's going on underneath that counts. Even though you've achieved so much, can you honestly say you're ever able to forget you were once a father? Can owning a fleet of cargo ships deflect the grief that sneaks up when you're not expecting it, and leaves you feeling as if you've been punched in the kidneys? If you were to take another wife, would that be enough to make you put away your memories and never think of Luciano again, or to forget that Chloe is the only woman you'll ever really love?''

Depressingly probing questions that would accept nothing but the truth for answers! He'd never forget his son, and Chloe…? Damn her, she was in his blood still, and no number of fresh transfusions seemed able to get rid of her.

So he stopped searching, stopped the interminable round of dating, and devoted himself to the one thing that never failed to bring him satisfaction: he made more money, with a series of daring investments that left his broker on the verge of a heart attack. Ironically, because it didn't much matter whether or not they paid off, they brought in handsome returns.

He bought himself a new Ferrari and a classic Bugatti.

''What's wrong with the Lamborghini?'' his sister Delia wanted to know. ''You can only drive one car at a time. Why own three?''

Annoyed, he said, ''Because I can afford them.''

He bought a place on the shores of Lake Garda, a mansion just outside Sirmione, formerly owned by an American movie star, and large enough that all four of his sisters and their families could stay there at one time.

''You already gave us that chalet in the Alps,'' Abree reminded him. ''Why this house, too, when we spend most of our time in Verona?''

''Does there have to be a reason?'' he snapped. ''Isn't it enough that I enjoy spending money on my family?''

It sounded all very fine in theory, but the fact remained that he gained no pleasure from any of it. Once upon a time, his ultimate dream had been to have more money than he could spend. Now that he'd got it, he found it was as empty as any other dream based on ignorance of what really counted in life.

CHAPTER TEN

April 14, the following year

SHE'D come to Verona as a young woman, been entranced by its history, and fallen in love in the summer shade of its medieval buildings. In the end, though, she'd endured some of her darkest hours there, and left it, vowing she'd never return. Yet the second she set foot on the ancient streets of *La Città degli Romeo e Giulietta* again, she felt she'd come home at last.

Nico hadn't the first idea of what lay in store. Indeed, she hardly knew herself. There'd been no contact between them since the previous August, when he'd unceremoniously turfed her out of the gardener's lodge, and out of his life. For all she knew, he might well be in love with someone else by now, and that would be a hard thing to accept. But Chloe was willing to deal with the possibility, if only to prove to herself and him that she was in control of her life and ready to confront whatever shape it might assume.

He was in town, she knew. Her mother had agreed to release that much information, along with his address. But Chloe didn't expect him to be home until the end of the business day, which was just as well. There was another place she needed to visit first, one she'd left too long neglected.

The churchyard lay bathed in sunshine. Making her way unerringly to her son's burial site, she crouched on the grass, a bouquet of spring flowers in her arms. She was not the first to stop by that day. Another arrangement, as freshly cut as hers, lay at the base of the simple marble plaque marking his place.

She traced her finger over his name, let it linger on her lips, then knelt, spread her hands palms down on the warm sod covering him and, for a little while, she cried. But not as she'd expected she might. There were no great, convulsive sobs, no feeling that her heart was being torn from her body. Rather, they were quiet, cleansing tears that ran down her face, and when they were done, she was left with a sense of peace she had not known in years.

She stayed there for nearly an hour, then walked back to where the taxi driver patiently waited, and directed him to take her into the center of town. Once there, she wandered the familiar streets and revisited some of the places to which Nico had introduced her, that passion-filled summer they met.

The *trattoria* in the sun-splashed square where they'd shared their first meal was there still, also the bakery above which he and his sisters had lived as children. The red geraniums his mother had loved bloomed in profusion from the window boxes, just as they had when she was alive.

The market in the *Piazza delle Erbe* bustled with its usual lively activity. He'd stolen two tangerines from a fruit stall, she remembered, and had laughed at her horrified gasp at his lawlessness.

After that, she strolled to the simple gray house at 23, *Via Cappello*—the famous House of Capulet, as it was still called, with its delicate balcony still hanging on the wall outside Juliet's window.

"You are my Giulietta," Nico had told her, the night they became lovers, "but our story will have a happier ending than hers. We'll live and love to a ripe old age together."

She'd believed him, and why not? Who could have foretold that it was their son who'd meet an early death, and not either of them, or that losing him would rob them of each other? But, God willing, it wasn't too late for them to make good on that early promise.

Dusk was falling when she finally found herself on the street where he lived, in an area of town clearly too high-rent for the average man. His front door was painted shiny black, with brass numbers marching vertically down its center panel. The white interior shutters at his windows were angled so that he could observe passers by without their being aware of his surveillance.

For a moment, the courage which had carried her this far evaporated. What if he happened to be looking out now, and saw her standing on the sidewalk? Would he be happy, angry, amused?

There was but one way to find out. Composing herself, she marched up the short walkway fronting the house and pressed the brass bell on the wall beside the door.

He took his time answering and looked none too pleased at being disturbed. When he saw who his visitor was, he wiped his face clean of all emotion and didn't betray by so much as the flicker of an eyelash his inner response to her presence. He merely stood there and waited for her to speak first.

Her own reaction was much more difficult to hide. Even though *she'd* been prepared to see *him*, her insides rolled over in one long, dizzying somersault. Her blood churned, her lungs froze, the *calzone* she'd eaten for lunch, nearly six hours before, rose up in her throat. As for her poor, beleaguered heart, it beat so hard and fast that the front of her blouse fluttered.

How long the silence lasted, she couldn't have said. All she knew was that she couldn't drag her eyes away from the sight of him. Even with a five o'clock shadow darkening his jaw, and his hair slightly mussed, he looked so handsome...so wary...so remote. And oh, so unmoved by his uninvited caller! Clearly, it would be up to her to break the ice—a metaphor, she thought dazedly, that all too well fit the occasion. His reception couldn't have been colder.

"Ciao!" she said, pasting what she hoped was a poised and relaxed smile on her face, but suspecting she looked as rattled as she surely sounded. "I guess I'm the last person you expected to see."

He inclined his head slightly, said, *"Sì,"* and continued to regard her without a trace of expression.

More discomfited by the second, she shifted from one foot to the other. "I...um, I arrived this morning."

No reaction, no curiosity, no interest. She might as well have been speaking in foreign tongues for all the acknowledgment she received.

Hating the desperation surely evident in her tone, she said, "I went to see Luciano today. Took some flowers to his grave, but there were others already there."

At last, a sign that he had heard, that he was listening. "I visited him myself, just this morning."

"You did?"

"I go every week, except when I'm away on business, and so do his aunts. We have not abandoned him.''

Though his tone remained neutral, the rebuke was unmistakable and it stung. ''And you think I have?''

''I try not to think of you at all,'' he replied cuttingly.

Oh, he was not going to make this easy on her! But then, why should he, when, in the past, she'd rebuffed his every attempt to help her? ''You're frequently in my thoughts, Nico.''

He shrugged, as if to say *And I should care?* ''What brings you to my door, Chloe?''

''I hoped we could talk. There's a lot I'd like to say to you.'' She glanced around at the darkening street, at the couple loitering a few houses away. ''But not out here where strangers might overhear. May I please come in?''

He lifted his shoulders in a faint shrug and stood back to allow her entry.

''Thank you.''

Stepping by him, so close that his dear, familiar scent pierced her senses, almost brought her to her knees. Clenching her hands around her purse, she stumbled into a wide entrance hall and waited, uncertain where he wished her to go next.

''I am in the middle of making myself something to eat. We will talk in the kitchen,'' he announced, and led the way past a formal dining room and long, elegant drawing room, to the rear of the house.

Hurrying to keep up with his impatient stride, she caught only a fleeting impression of the decor, but the compilation of polished floors, thick, pale rugs, and silk-paneled walls suggested discreet expense combined with flawless taste.

The kitchen might have been lifted straight from the pages of a glossy magazine. Sleek built-in appliances, lacquered cabinets and granite counters swept around three sides of one half of the vast room stretching the full width of the house. The fourth, containing a free-standing breakfast bar and two stools, separated the working area from a family room furnished with deep, comfortable sofas and an entertainment unit. A brick-faced fireplace filled the far wall.

Gesturing to the open bottle of Bardolino on the bar, he said with chilly, perfect courtesy, "I was about to pour myself a glass of wine. Do you care to join me?"

"Oh, yes. *Please!*" Although she didn't normally resort to alcohol to steady her nerves, at that precise moment, she'd have been happy to take a straw, stick it in the neck of the bottle, and drain the entire contents in one go. She hadn't expected he'd burst into song and dance in unabashed pleasure at the sight of her, but nor had she been prepared for such a stony, indifferent reception.

Unaware—or more likely uncaring of the anxiety ravaging her, he reached up and removed two long-stemmed glasses from a brass rack suspended above the bar. "What is it you came to say, Chloe?" he inquired politely, pouring the Bardolino.

"I hardly know where to begin." She climbed on one of the stools and cradled the bowl of her glass between her hands. Very fine crystal for everyday use, she noted absently. "After our last meeting, I'm not even sure *how* to begin."

"Try speaking plainly. I assume something more

pressing than visiting our son's grave compelled you to travel halfway around the world.''

"You're not making this easy for me, Nico.''

"I'm under no obligation to do so. You're the one paying the unexpected visit, not I. The ball, as they say, lies in your court.''

She took a deep breath, followed it with a fortifying mouthful of wine, and plunged in. "I wanted to tell you, to your face, that you were right. My marrying Baron would have been a monumental mistake. I canceled the wedding the day before it was supposed to take place—the same day that you left the country without a word. I came to see you afterward, but I was too late. If you'd waited just a few hours more—''

"There was no point,'' he interrupted. "We'd reached a dead end.''

"Yes. At that point, we had. But I've done a lot of soul-searching since then, Nico, and I thought...I hoped we might try to find a way out of that dead end, and start afresh.''

"It took you eight months to decide that?'' he scoffed. "What happened, Chloe? Did you run out of other options and decide that making do with me was preferable to having no one at all?''

"No!'' she gasped, recoiling from such a low blow. "You made it clear enough that you had no use for an emotional cripple, so what would have been the point in my showing up sooner?''

"No point at all,'' he said flatly. "I meant what I said.''

"As did I, a moment ago,'' she returned, with a flash of anger. "But I'm beginning to wonder why I bothered. If I've left it too late and you've moved on, just say so. I'm not going to slit my wrists in your bathroom and leave you to clean up the mess. I'll be hurt and disappointed, but I've survived worse, and I'll survive this.''

He leaned against the other side of the bar, hands lying flat on the tiled surface, arms braced. The knot in his silk tie hung loose, the top button of his shirt was undone, yet his pose was anything but casual. Although his dark glance never wavered, the air around him fairly crackled with tension. Finally, sounding almost ashamed, he said, ''Did I really call you an emotional cripple?''

''Not in so many words, perhaps, but that was the message I received.''

He chewed that over for a minute or so, then said, ''If being with me was really so important, why take a chance on waiting this long to say so? It's been almost a year, Chloe. How do you know I'm not involved with someone else?''

''I don't,'' she admitted, ''and the thought that you might be, has haunted me for months. But if I'd acted on impulse and come to you right after I ended things with Baron, would you have believed I was sincere?''

''Probably not. I'd have thought you were running *away* from the situation you'd left behind, rather than running *to* me.''

''Exactly. Which is why I took as long as I needed to heal myself first, even though that meant taking the chance that a third party might lay claim to your affections.'' She stared at the dark red wine in her glass, unable to meet his gaze and painfully aware that she sounded more as if she were presenting a case in court, than speaking from the heart to the man she loved. ''Is that what's happened, Nico? Is there another woman in your life?''

''There have been others in the months since I saw you last,'' he said.

Pain clutched at her heart and her palms went clammy with sweat. Worse, she knew a sudden dire need to use the toilet. Her bladder had always been her barometer for measuring mental stress, and at that moment it felt ready to burst. ''And now?''

He swung away and went to the stove where a pot simmered. ''I'm making fish soup,'' he said. ''If you'd like to stay, there's enough for two.''

If it wasn't the answer she'd been hoping for, it wasn't an outright rejection, either, and at that point she was prepared to take whatever he was willing to offer. ''Is it your mother's recipe?''

''*Sì.* ''

''Then I'd love to.''

He flung her a glance which seemed not quite as chilly as its predecessors. There was even the faintest trace of amusement in his voice when he said, ''I can't help noticing that you're squirming around on that stool, Chloe. Will it help relieve your discomfort if I tell you the powder room is just to the left of the front door?''

She slithered off the stool with more speed than grace. ''You know me too well,'' she said, and made a beeline down the hall.

She wasn't the only one who needed a few moments alone. He was in pretty rough shape himself. Finding her on his doorstep had rocked him badly. He'd had the devil of a time subduing the burst of hope which had flared through him. Maintaining an impassive front had stretched his control past human limits, but he'd played similar scenes with her too often in the past, not to be cautious now.

His experience last summer had taught him that she might turn to him when she was uncertain, when she was in a bind, when she needed to be rescued. Otherwise, she stayed away. That was enough for him to remain on his guard until he had solid reason to think this time would be any different.

There was a fine distinction, though, between holding something of himself in reserve, and being churlish. Whatever her real motive for seeking him out now, she didn't deserve the ugly treatment he'd meted out. But the sad truth was, she terrified the wits out of him.

He could deal with thugs if he had to, wasn't the least bit afraid to use his fists or whatever else came to hand, if he must. But her big, anxious eyes and soft trembling mouth unmanned him in a way that was downright embarrassing.

She could fell him with a glance, a word, a sigh. One touch of her hand, a single faint whiff of her perfume, and he turned to putty, any memory of other women blasted to kingdom come so completely that, on pain of death, he couldn't name one of them.

He drained his glass and debated pouring himself something stronger. He wanted to believe what she'd told him just a few minutes earlier. *Dio*, he'd never wanted anything as badly in his life! But he'd learned too much about his own frailty simply to take her at her word. He had to be sure; had to drive her to her own limits before he could be certain she wouldn't push him past his.

"Let me do that," she said, coming back to the kitchen as he was tossing dressing over mixed salad greens.

"No," he said, the jutting angle of his shoulder denying her the right to invade his space. "You're a guest here."

"Well, at least let me set the table."

"We'll eat at the bar."

Her sigh penetrated his shirt and rippled warmly up his spine. *Dio!*

"I thought we were making progress, Nico."

"Perhaps so," he acknowledged, steeling himself to remain distant, "but one small step at a time, yes? Where are you staying?"

"At the *Due Torri Baglioni.*"

"I used to wait on the street outside that hotel in the summer, and offer to act as a guide to tourists— one of my more enterprising adolescent get-rich-quick schemes."

"Was it successful?"

"No. The people who could afford to stay there weren't interested in having a fourteen-year-old tow them around town in a homemade cart attached to his old bike." He shook his head and laughed bitterly. "Now, I could buy the entire place for pocket change, yet in some ways I'm no better off than I was twenty years ago."

"I guess we've both learned that happiness isn't something that can be acquired."

"Have we?" He pinned her in a searching gaze. "Have *you*, Chloe?"

"Yes," she said, on another sigh. "No one else can

give it to us. It comes from within ourselves, or not at all.''

He placed the salad on the bar, and turned to give the fish soup one last stir.

She was saying all the right things, but how deeply did she believe them? ''Are you happy?''

She gave the question a moment's thought. ''I'm content,'' she finally said. ''I'm at peace with myself, and with the past, and that's worth a lot to me. If what I have now is the best I'm ever going to get, I can live with it. But I'd be happier if…'' She drifted into thoughtful silence and stared at the darkening window.

''Yes?'' he prompted. ''If what?''

''I've tried to undo most of my mistakes…all except one, really. I have to try to put that right before I can say I'm truly satisfied.'' She stopped again and bit her lip. ''You know why I'm here, Nico. I've already spelled it out once. But if you need to hear me say it again, I will. I'll say it as many times as it takes for you to believe me. *I want you to give us another chance. I want us to be happy together.*''

''On what terms?''

''No terms,'' she said. ''I'm offering unconditional surrender.''

''And if I tell you that I cannot be quite so generous? That I would exact a price?''

''You want more children.'' She inclined her head. ''I know.''

''I want the possibility of such. A fresh start to me means giving everything a second chance, and if that should mean more children, well—''

''I know, and I agree.''

''Just like that?'' He tilted his head and regarded

her askance. "You must forgive me, Chloe, if I'm somewhat cynical of such a complete turnaround. Is it perhaps that you're so eager for us to be a couple again that you will agree to anything now, only to change your mind once you are assured that my heart is yours to trample on as you see fit?"

"No, it isn't," she replied, her eyes fixed on him unblinkingly. "But I don't expect you to take my word on that, just because I say so. I'm not asking to move in here and pick up where we left off. I'm not asking you to marry me. But I *am* hoping that, in time, you'll come to trust me enough to allow for both to become a possibility."

"How do I do that, with you living thousands of kilometers away? A long-distance relationship isn't my style, *cara*. Or have you forgotten the last time we tried such an arrangement?"

"Hardly," she said, with the first inkling of a smile she'd shown all evening. "The phone bills were astronomical!"

"So how, then, do we enter into this experiment?"

"By my living here."

"Here?"

"Not *here* here," she amended. "Here in Verona. I'm back to stay, Nico, whether or not you want me."

"You know that I want you, *mia strega piccola!* That is one thing that has never changed. But what you're proposing is not practical. You have a career."

"Had," she said. "I *had* a career until I realized that I'd be better off solving my own marital problems, instead of other people's. I resigned from the law firm, terminated the lease on my condominium, packed up the things most important to me—family photographs,

a few heirlooms, my clothes, that kind of thing—and had them shipped over. They should be here by the end of next week. Meanwhile, I'll stay at the hotel until I find an apartment. I've already been to the police station and applied for my temporary Resident's Permit. That's good for three months. If, at the end of that time, you're still undecided about us, I'll apply for a permanent certificate of residence and a work permit.''

''You cannot practice law in Italy.''

''Certainly I can, as long as I meet national standards and pass the bar exam. But I'm hoping that won't be necessary.''

She sounded so sure of herself, so full of confidence, but he saw the uncertainty in her eyes and didn't have the heart to leave her dangling a moment longer. ''No wife of mine will work to support herself,'' he informed her severely. ''She will devote herself to her husband and children.''

A flush rose up her face. Tears filmed her eyes. ''Exactly what are you saying, Nico?''

''That if you still choose to do so, you have come home, Chloe. At long last, we will become a couple again, and we will make it official with all due speed.''

''Are you saying that we'll be married?''

He threw up his hands in frustration. ''*Sì*, we will be married, if not tomorrow, then the day after! How much more plainly must I put it, woman?''

''Well, you could show me, instead of shouting at me.''

''And how would you like me to do that?''

She shrugged. ''At the very least, you could kiss me.''

He came around the breakfast bar, to where she sat perched on the high stool. "And at the very most?" he said, daring at last to touch her.

"Oh well," she murmured, batting her lashes provocatively, "that's really up to you. You're the boss, after all."

"Will you give that to me in writing, *Signorina L'Avvocato,* to make a legally binding agreement of it?"

"Why not? I'm giving you everything else that I am."

He gripped her shoulders and looked deep into her eyes, more beautiful and blue than the Adriatic in high summer. He saw truth there, and trust, and belief in the future. "That is good," he murmured, "because without you, *la mia inamorata,* I am nothing."

"I've been running for such a long time, for years away from sadness and loss, and, in the last few months, toward hope and happiness," she confessed, leaning into his strength and letting him bear her weight, just as she used to, before they'd allowed tragedy to tear them apart. "To feel your arms around me again and know I've finally come back to the place where I belong…" She bowed her head and pressed her face against his shirtfront a moment. "Nico, you can't begin to guess how good it feels to leave the shadows behind and step into the sunlight again."

"I understand better than you might think, my angel," he said, the slow burn of desire simmering through his veins growing fiercer by the second. "I let perfection slip through my fingers when I lost you, and came close to losing my mind also. Now that you're back where you belong, I'll never let you go again."

CHAPTER ELEVEN

THEY forgot the fish soup was still simmering on the stove, that the salad, left sitting far too long at room temperature, grew warm and limp and inedible.

"Didn't you say we should take small steps?" she asked, as he carried her up the stairs.

"Impossible," he laughed. "A man my size doesn't know how."

"But I didn't come prepared for seduction, Nico."

He stopped at the threshold to his bedroom, a slight frown casting a cloud over his smile. "If you're worried you'll get pregnant, don't be. I will protect you. There'll be no baby conceived tonight, and you may be assured I do not intend to pressure you on this, Chloe. We will know when the time is right."

"You don't understand," she said. "I'm not talking about contraception. If I conceive tonight, it will be because it was meant to be. But..." She touched her blouse, the wrinkled cotton of her skirt. "I would have liked to be prettier for you. After all the mistakes and near misses of last summer, I'd have liked our first time together in our new life to be romantic and perfect."

"Cara," he said, "in my eyes you have never been more beautiful and nothing can mar the perfection of this night. But if more romance is what you need, then more you shall have. What will it take? Tell me, and I'll make it happen."

"Oh, nothing too elaborate," she said softly, winding her arms more tightly around his neck and pressing a kiss to his mouth. "A hot bath would do it very nicely."

He set her on her feet and steered her toward a door on the other side of the room. "My home, such as it is, and everything in it, is yours to share, Chloe. Help yourself. I'll be here waiting when you're ready."

She was in no hurry to rejoin him, not because she needed to be sure the next step she'd take was the right one. She'd never been more certain of anything in her life. It was that she wanted to make each minute last; preserve forever in her memory each perfect second.

While the bath filled, she shampooed her hair in the glass-enclosed shower stall, and took deep delight in the implied intimacy of using *his* shampoo, *his* towels. In lieu of perfumed bath crystals, she added a dollop of his Alfred Sung aftershave to the bathwater, soaped the sponge which knew every long muscle, every hard plane of his body, and let it caress her own body until not an inch of her skin was left untouched.

Finally, she slid down in the tub deeply enough for tiny waves to ripple at her throat and fragrant steam to curl around her face, and allowed herself the pleasure of contemplating the night ahead.

Pure bliss and simmering expectation made for a potent cocktail, and when he rapped on the door several minutes later to inquire, "Did you drown, my angel?" she was more than ready for the next stage in the ritual of their renewed courtship.

Swathed in a velvety bath sheet, she returned to the bedroom, but stopped short at the sight awaiting her. He hadn't been twiddling his thumbs during her absence. Pinpoints of soft light glimmered from more than a dozen tealights floating in crystal brandy snifters stationed on every flat surface about the room. Creamy pink rose petals, their scent so sweet that they must have been plucked from their stems only minutes before, lay scattered in a path from her feet to the turned-back covers on the bed.

He stood by the window, stripped naked except for the towel slung around his waist. His hair was damp and even though the candles cast only a muted glow, she could see that he'd shaved. "If you'd told me you were going to bathe, too," she said, resorting to the mundane because the fact that he was there, in the flesh and not just in her dreams, rendered her almost mindless, "we could have done it together."

His low laugh floated through the night and wrapped itself around her. "A cold shower for my ladylove? I think not! But we *will* make love together."

Everything was so utterly idyllic, so beyond even her most optimistic hopes, that she wanted to pinch herself. "We really are here together, aren't we, Nico? This isn't a figment of my imagination?"

"We are indeed here, *mia moglie,* starting over as I've so often prayed we might. I thought of putting champagne on ice, to celebrate the occasion," he said huskily, his eyes devouring her, "but I want you to come to me with every sense alive, with every beat of your heart aware of the step we're about to take. I don't want you to wake up tomorrow filled with any regrets."

She'd wondered if she'd feel shy; if time and their painful history might make it awkward for her to relax with him. She had not expected he might be the one needing reassurance. He was so confident always, so positive he could turn every situation in his favor. That he harbored even the smallest doubt of his ability to do so tonight melted her already willing heart.

"There'll be no regrets, my love," she said, going to him without hesitation, aware of the towel unraveling as she moved until, just as she reached him, it fell away entirely. "No second thoughts, no changing my mind at the last second."

His smile undid her. For once it was not brash and beguiling, but slow and so tender that it left her weak at the knees. He loosened the knot anchoring his own towel and let it fall to join hers on the floor. "How can I be sure?" he said.

She placed her hands on his chest. Splayed her fingers to discover his flat, dark nipples. Bent her head and kissed the swell of muscle underlying his smooth olive skin. Grazed her cheek against the dusting of black hair shadowing his breastbone. "By this?" she whispered.

He might have been carved from marble for all the response he made. Only his magnificently aroused flesh betrayed his tortured pleasure.

Spurred to a daring beyond anything she'd attempted before, she slid her arms around him and traced her fingers down his spine to his buttocks, all the while following a path to his waist with her tongue. "Or this?"

Encouraged by his barely suppressed moan, she pressed a wet, openmouthed kiss at his navel, then continued lower to string feather-light kisses in the narrow triangle formed by his hips.

The breath hissed between his lips. His fingers knotted in her hair.

Slipping her hand between his thighs, she cradled the vulnerable cluster hidden there, then took the silken tip of him in her mouth.

"Enough!" he groaned, shuddering as violently as if an earthquake had struck. "I am convinced!"

She was trembling herself, by then; aching and eager all over, and so weak with longing that she'd have collapsed at his feet had he not drawn her up until she was imprinted against him, inch for inch.

How joyfully her body remembered his; how easily the two melded together, soft feminine warmth and unyielding male strength in perfect harmony. His arms enfolded her, tight and possessive, and when at last he kissed her, as if he could never get enough of the taste and texture of her mouth, the hell of their long separation faded away, and left heaven hovering so close, she could almost touch it.

She had no clear recollection of how they came to be lying together on the petal-strewn bed. All she knew was that the erotic play of his hands at her breasts, her waist, her hips, sent sensation pooling low in her body. An undulating rhythm, the forerunner of complete surrender, pulsed so insistently within her that all he had to do was touch his mouth to her core, flick once with his tongue, and the world as she knew it fell away.

Grasping and clutching at him, she submitted as wave upon wave of sheer ecstasy washed over her. She heard her own moans echo inside her head. Heard Nico calling her name.... "Chloe, Chloe...*tesoro!*" followed by a string of other words, erotic words uttered in Italian, but so full of unrestrained passion that there was no mistaking their meaning.

When at last, he slid inside her, he did so with the reverence of a man entering a sacred temple, and with each slow penetration, he soothed away the last rough, hurting edges of her soul.

Opening her eyes, she stared up at him. The candlelight painted shifting shadows of bronze and umber and gold over his skin, and filled his eyes with dark fire. "I love you, Nico," she breathed, locking her gaze in his.

Buried thick inside her, he increased the tempo of his loving, his thrusts deep and urgent, slick and fast. And she, caught up in his fierce possession of everything she was, felt herself lured a second time, ever closer to the merciless whirlpool of capitulation.

Defying her every attempt to subdue it, the pleasure swept her in ever diminishing circles, then sucked her without mercy into its bottomless depths. She screamed softly, blinded by its power, deaf to all but the blood drumming in her ears, and aware only of the hot spurt of Nico's seed running free inside her.

He filled not just the yearning in her body, but all the empty spaces in her heart. For the first time in over four years, she felt whole again.

Devastated by the emotional catharsis, she clung to him and burst into tears. He understood the reason, held her safe in his arms as the storm raged, and smothered her cries with kisses until she grew calm again.

Later, lying sated and sleepy with her head on his shoulder and the moon beaming full through the window, she murmured dreamily, "It feels as if we were never apart."

"Darling," he said, holding her closer, "in my heart we never were divorced. It just took me a while to convince you of it."

CHAPTER TWELVE

THEY decided on a summer wedding. "But something small," Nico insisted, afraid Chloe would overtax herself. "Just family and a few very close friends."

The problem lay in the fact that he had such a large family and so many friends, all of whom had missed seeing him get married the first time around. But in the end, they pared the guest list down to forty adults and thirteen children.

"Thirteen and a third, if truth be told," Nico whispered the week before the wedding, placing his hand possessively over Chloe's womb, as they lay in bed in the Verona house, with the moon beaming full through the window on their naked bodies. "But that will remain our little secret for a few more weeks."

She had never known such tranquil happiness.

"Do not concern yourself, *Signora*," the obstetrician had told her, just that morning. "The odds of your suffering another tragedy such as you knew with your first child are so small as to be negligible. There is every reason to believe this child will grow up to be as strong and healthy as his father."

"And if it's a girl?" she'd asked, smiling.

His eyes had twinkled. "She will be beautiful like her mother, and before she is out of the cradle, her father will be gray-haired and exhausted from fighting off the boys."

Of course, Jacqueline and Charlotte flew over for the wedding, arriving just two days ahead of time.

"Long enough for us to recover from jet lag, but not long enough for us to do any damage," Charlotte explained mischievously. "We didn't think it wise to come any sooner, not after the way we meddled before and ended up making such a mess of everything."

But nothing and no one could dim Chloe's radiance, or spoil things for her. Nico's sisters had welcomed her back into the family with more warmth than she felt she deserved, and showered her with love, throwing themselves wholeheartedly into the wedding preparations, and providing unconditional support of the marriage.

"I don't need to ask if you're sure you know what you're doing this time," Jacqueline said fondly when Chloe came to help her settle in and unpack her suitcase. "Your smile's enough to blind a person! But I don't mind admitting, your grandmother and I had more than a few sleepless nights after you left Vancouver and came here without so much as a hint of how Nico would receive you. We're so delighted it all worked out for you, darling. You and Nico are meant to be together, and we know you'll both be very happy."

Although she and her husband came for the wedding, Monica begged off acting as matron of honor because she was nearly eight months pregnant with her third child, "and I'd need a tent to cover this," she said wryly, stroking her swollen abdomen.

But there was no shortage of flower girls offering to take her place: Nico's six nieces, ranging from two to five-and-a-half, couldn't wait to dress up like princesses and steal the show.

Disappointed, the nephews complained that everyone liked girls best, and gave them all the special favors. "Not this time," their uncle told them. "You boys will be my groomsmen—at least, those of you who aren't still in diapers—and it'll be your job to keep the girls in line."

He and Chloe chose the mansion on Lake Garda as the place to hold the wedding. "Outdoors, if possible," she suggested. "Down by the water on the lower terrace, for the ceremony, and on the upper one, right outside the main salon, for the reception. It'll be more convenient there for the caterers."

"Whatever you want, my angel," Nico said, seducing her with his smile in full view of anyone who happened to be watching. "And we can host the entire occasion indoors if it rains. The house is certainly big enough."

"You couldn't have chosen a more beautiful setting," her mother sighed, leaning against the fat stone balusters forming the wall between land and lake, on the wedding eve, and gazing out at the mountains beyond the old town. "Just look at that view! It's like something out of a fairy tale. Oh, I hope the weather cooperates tomorrow."

It did. Not a breath of wind marred the surface of the water, or disturbed the path of rose petals—creamy pink to match Chloe's ankle-length dress, though why she chose that particular color scheme was something known only to her and Nico!—strewn from the French doors of the house by the flower girls.

Adorable in white organdy with coronets of pink

rosebuds, they meandered along the flagstone path to Franck's *Fantasie,* played by Nico's brother-in-law, Hector. The concert grand had been rolled out to the upper terrace earlier by the crew who'd also erected a flower-draped arch on the terrace, where the couple would exchange their vows.

The groomsmen, meanwhile, stood at attention beside Nico, taking their roles very seriously. Their mission earlier had been to make sure bride and groom didn't see each other before the ceremony, and the boys had adhered to the task religiously.

Chloe chose the *Theme* from Tchaikovsky's *Fifth Symphony* to herald her own entrance. Although the women grew a little misty-eyed when she stepped out of the house, her face shaded by a wide-brimmed cream hat trimmed with pink roses, their tears turned to laughter when the youngest flower girl, Lisabetta, already bored with the proceedings, wandered away from the wedding party and plunked herself down on the lawn to pick daisies.

Chloe knew there was speculation among the immediate family that perhaps she was in the early stages of pregnancy. She'd lost her breakfast, seven mornings running, and looked, according to her future sisters-in-law, as if a stiff breeze might blow her away, "the way a woman often does during her first trimester."

They'd find out soon enough that they were right. Today, though, was not about a baby, but about Nico and her. Indeed, there might just as well have been no guests there to witness the marriage, for all the attention she spared them. She had eyes only for her groom, and he for her. The priest had to cough twice before they tore their gazes away from one another and turned to hear what he had to say.

Fifteen minutes later, they were again man and wife in the eyes of God, and the State. Just as well. Neither Nico's family nor hers would have looked kindly on her giving birth to an illegitimate baby. As for keeping her pregnancy secret, given her new husband's protective concern for his bride and the way he hovered over her, he might just as well have announced the news to the entire congregation.

But then, she was just as solicitous of him, reaching up to secure his rose boutonniere more firmly to the lapel of his cream jacket, and smooth her hand down his cheek as she whispered, "I love you," before they exchanged their first married kiss in nearly half a decade.

And what a kiss it was, long and sweet enough to make up for the arid years they'd been apart. Tender enough to make the men smile and the women dab their eyes again.

The wedding supper, held on the upper terrace, began as the sun started to sink behind the mountains. Kerosene torches illuminated the scene for the waiters serving a feast of seafood chicchetti, grilled swordfish, black lobster ravioli with a cognac basil cream sauce, crab gnocchi and other delicious pastas, all accompanied by a selection of the finest regional wines.

The dessert buffet which followed rivaled anything the world's most renowned restaurants might offer. Tiramisu, of course, and zabaglione; delicate Venetian pastries, and assorted fresh fruits and cheeses. And for the children, six different flavors of gelato.

"Our arteries aren't thanking us for this," Jacqueline

told Charlotte, as they sampled the decadent confections, "but we'll worry about that tomorrow."

Throughout the lengthy banquet, a pair of musicians wandered among the candlelit tables and provided dreamy background music on a mandolin and accordion. There was much laughter and singing, champagne toasts and many long speeches, and a handful of telegrams conveying good wishes and congratulations from distant friends, including one from Baron. He wasn't able to attend because he was in the midst of moving across country, to take up the position of senior partner in his grandfather's old law firm. Mrs. Prescott, Chloe thought, amused, would surely approve.

Later, with the moon carving a silver swath over the lake, and the children put to bed, Nico took Chloe in his arms for the first dance. The mandolin plucked at the heartstrings of all who watched, the accordion sighed; *Non Dimenticar…Mala Femana…Arrivederci Roma…Volare….*

His ring warm on her finger, his arms firm around her still-slender waist, Chloe gazed into her husband's eyes and saw a future full of promise. She knew with absolute conviction that although most times would be "for better," if "for worse" happened anyway, she and Nico would face it together.

This time *was* forever.

Mamma Mia!

Reader favorite

Emma Darcy

brings you the next installment in

THE ITALIAN'S STOLEN BRIDE

June 2005, #2469

They're tall, dark…and ready to marry!

Pick up the next story in
this great new miniseries…pronto!

Available where Harlequin books are sold.

If you enjoyed what you just read,
then we've got an offer you can't resist!

Take 2 bestselling love stories FREE!

Plus get a FREE surprise gift!

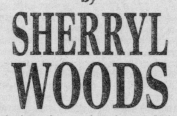
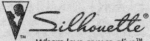

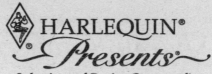

Seduction and Passion Guaranteed!

He's proud, passionate, primal—dare she surrender to the sheikh?

Feel warm desert winds blowing through your hair, and experience hot sexy nights with a handsome, irresistible sheikh. If you love our heroes of the sand, look for more stories in this enthralling miniseries, coming soon.

Coming in June 2005:

THE SHEIKH'S VIRGIN
by *Jane Porter*
#2473

Available only from Harlequin Presents®.